DESERT VENOM

A COLD WAR NOVELLA

JAMES BLATCH

Desert Venom by James Blatch published by Vivid Dog Limited, 4a Church Street, Market Harborough, LE16 7AA, UK

ISBN: 978-1-8384894-4-1

For David, my brother.

1

The airstream tore at the canopy in an angry howl.

Rob estimated they had six seconds before smashing into the desert floor.

He snatched a glance at the attitude indicator. Sixty degrees nose down.

The notes said forty-five for a rocket attack.

Even if they abandoned the dive now, he doubted they would have enough height to pull up.

"A bit longer," Bunny said from the right-hand seat, sounding for all the world as if he were on a country walk and fancied staying out, despite the hint of rain in the air.

Rob's fingers twitched. He fought every fibre in his body to grab the control column and wrench it back.

His first flight on his first squadron was about to be his last.

He could now read the stencilled writing on the side of the target; a derelict tank. Its tracks hanging off after decades of abuse from the pilots of RAF Habbaniya.

Rob's turn at the controls was supposed to come after the demonstration from his flight commander. But all

Bunny had demonstrated, as far as Rob could see, was how to ignore every line in the pilot's notes and fly with reckless abandon.

It was far from the structured, methodical approach he'd grown used to during eighteen months of flying training back home.

He'd noticed a few of the chaps laugh when his flight commander was allocated to him, the previous evening.

Flight Lieutenant 'Bunny' Pater-Smith.

'*The Daredevil of two-one-seven*', someone whispered to him.

But this wasn't daring. This was suicide.

"Nearly there," Bunny said, drawing out the words.

The tank filled the windshield. Rob could stand it no longer.

A sudden realisation; *this must be a test.*

He grabbed the stick, pulled it back, and with his other hand, advanced the throttle to max power.

"What the hell?" Bunny shouted. He briefly fought back with his side of the controls, but Rob held the stick firm.

The view ahead filled with brown desert. The nose started to rise, but they were still descending.

"Shit," Rob said.

Too much speed.

Too much angle.

Too late.

On instinct, Rob threw an arm in front of his face.

Bunny snorted and took control again. The silver fighter skipped over the flat ground, missing contact by a few feet.

They sailed up into the cloudless Iraqi sky.

He slowly put his arms down; Bunny stared at him.

They were pressed together in the side-by-side cockpit. Bunny's eyes bulging over his oxygen mask.

"Never touch my controls again, you snivelling little bastard."

"Yes, sir," Rob said, bowing his head.

Bunny levelled the aircraft and banked to the north, pointing the Vampire at Habbaniya.

"And that, Flying Officer May, is a fail."

2

They unstrapped from the two-seat trainer and walked in silence past the long line of shiny, single-seat Venoms, the aircraft Rob was supposed to be flying after a successful dual check flight.

Now he was unsure whether he was still an RAF pilot.

His first flight out of training, on his first front-line posting, ending with a royal bollocking from a Second World War veteran and highly experienced jet pilot.

What was I thinking?

"What the hell were you thinking?" Bunny said, finally breaking the silence.

"I thought I was saving us."

Bunny stopped and moved in front of him. "I don't need saving."

"Yes, Bunny. I just thought—"

"You're not here to think, May. You're a child in this place. Remember that." Bunny's eyes narrowed. For a second, Rob thought he might strike him.

But something changed in his demeanour. His expression softened. A hint of a smile formed on his thin lips.

He looked into Rob's eyes and raised his hand to his head. Rob flinched.

Bunny laughed. "I'm not going to hit you, May."

The Iraqi heat was oppressive. Bunny's hand slid across Rob's forehead, unsticking the hair and reshaping his parting.

"We all make mistakes, May," he whispered before turning and continuing his walk back to the squadron hangar.

Rob stood, holding his silver flying helmet and oxygen mask, not understanding what had just happened.

He walked after his strange flight commander but stayed a couple of steps behind.

Waiting for them at the end of the line of 217 Squadron Venoms was a local man in a uniform Rob didn't recognise, a slanted hat that reminded him of the Anzacs.

Bunny handed the man his flying kit.

"Back to the hatch, Asu. No more flights today, and hand this paperwork to the duty sergeant, please."

"Yes, sir," the man said and headed for the offices nestled at the base of the large green hangar.

Bunny didn't follow him. Instead, he stood still, apparently staring at the rest of RAF Habbaniya.

Rob stayed a yard behind him, not daring to move.

After a few seconds of awkward nothing, Bunny turned to face him.

"Are you married, May?"

"No, Bunny."

"Girlfriend?"

"No."

"Then what were you trying to live for?"

Rob stared back. "I'm sorry?"

"Don't be a fucking coward, May."

Before Rob could reply, his flight commander walked away.

3

Inside the offices, Rob returned his flying equipment to the hatch and filled out his after-flight paperwork.

The place was bustling. As soon as he'd arrived, less than twenty-four hours ago, there were rumours they were about to move. Some contingency plan for a fast escape.

Everyone seemed to have twenty additional tasks, and no one had time for a new boy.

A week ago, he'd been walking along Saunton Sands with the close friends he'd made through training. Suddenly, it was at an end. Wings were awarded, and the pals were sent to the four corners.

He considered himself one of the lucky ones, a glamorous posting in single-seaters. The less lucky ended up in Meteors at Church Fenton, or worse, Transport Command.

He didn't feel lucky now.

The pen was heavy in his hand as he sat at a table and completed the entry in his logbook.

Dual check (fail).

"May, is it?"

A shadow fell over him. Rob got up to see a tall pilot with blond hair and a blue spotted cravat. A cigarette was stuck to his bottom lip.

"Yes, sir."

"No need to call me sir. I'm a flight lieutenant." He removed the cigarette and stuck out a hand. "Clive Nuffield."

Rob shook it. "They call me Rob."

"Yes, well, we'll come up with a nickname for you at some point. How was your first flight at Habbaniya?"

As he asked the question, another pilot nearby turned to hear the answer.

"Erm, I believe Flight Lieutenant Pater-Smith failed me."

The two men burst out laughing.

"You got Bunny! They finally found someone to fly with him?"

Nuffield slapped his shoulder. "Just so you know, as a two-one-seven flight commander, Bunny had the grand total of one pilot, and he's fled back to England on some pretence or other. So now he has you. I'm only sorry me and Tilly have our hands full with the rest."

"Right," Rob said.

"Keep your back against the wall, old boy," the other pilot said.

Rob noticed a brief but clear look of admonishment from Nuffield to the other man, as if he'd spoken out of turn.

He turned back to Rob. "Anyway, it's good of you to take a bullet for the team."

"Thank you," Rob said.

"Now, are you sorted for tonight?"

"Tonight?"

"Formal dining-in. Guest of honour. Prince Nuri."

Rob stared.

"Brother of King Faisal the Second. The man can't keep

away at the moment. Anyway, Bunny should have told you. You must have black tie."

"Black tie? I have the RAF blue."

Nuffield shook his head. "Not good enough. Must be black here. They take this stuff seriously."

"Nuff!" Someone called across the room; Nuffield looked around. "You're needed, now." A moustachioed pilot pointed to a side office.

"Got to go," Nuffield said as he walked off. "But find a bloody black tie. Or get a felt tip." He laughed at his own joke as he disappeared into the meeting.

Rob slowly closed his logbook and picked up his chart.

The pilot on the next table was busy working on a plan.

"Excuse me. You don't know where I could get a black bow tie, do you?"

The man laughed. "Sorry, chap. I've just the one. I doubt you'll find anyone with a spare. Better try the tailors." He glanced at his watch. "But hurry."

The man went back to his paperwork, leaving Rob standing alone.

A failed first flight, and now the prospect of turning up to a station-wide dining-in night with the wrong-coloured bow tie, which would probably be seen as the greater sin.

If the transport aircraft that delivered him to Iraq were still here, he would have asked to get back on.

After completing his admin, he pushed the door open to the outside world. The air was dry; his throat felt scratchy.

The wind was getting up and Rob raised a hand to block the glare of the lowering sun, as he looked for someone who might help him.

His eyes rested on Asu, who he assumed was Bunny's batman. Rob had no personal experience with batmen, but from what he understood, they were the sort who looked after uniform.

Asu was talking with two other local men in similar uniforms. He seemed to be organising them, giving them instructions. They looked on attentively and turned to march away when Asu, who was wearing corporal stripes, dismissed them.

As the conversation finished, Rob approached Asu, but he looked preoccupied and strode away quickly. Rob had to break into a jog to catch him.

"Excuse me."

Asu spun on his heels. He gave a smart salute. "Yes, sir? Flying Officer May."

"Gosh. You know my name?"

"Yes, sir. It was on the form."

Rob winced. The form that said he'd failed his check-ride.

"Yes, well, I have a problem. I need a black bow tie. Cummerbund, too, I think. Do you know where the supplies are?"

Asu nodded. "Sir, uniform supplies are next to the medical centre near the main gate, but I do not think they have what you are looking for. You must visit Cheapside."

"Cheapside?"

"Sir, it is a road where the tailors are, but it is past the Levies' streets. That way."

Rob admired Asu's good English. He looked to be in his forties and seemed to have quite an authority about him.

"I don't know what that means, but can you give me directions?"

Asu shook his head. "No, sir. You must not go now. Not alone. It is . . ." He paused. "It is not advisable."

"Is it not on the RAF station? It is rather urgent."

"Sir, it is in the greater part of RAF Habbaniya, but the Iraqi police now come in, and many men who do not work here are there."

"Right," Rob said, still not seeing a major issue.

Two more men in the same uniform approached, looking serious. Asu glanced at them.

"Sir, I have much to do. Will you kindly let me go now?"

"Yes, yes. Of course. Thank you, Asu."

He watched as Asu gave the other two men orders. One of them wore sergeant stripes. Everyone seemed to defer to Asu.

Rob walked off in the direction Asu had indicated. He'd be damned if he was going to fail a check-flight and then be made a laughing stock on his first day.

If this place Cheapside was in the greater part of RAF Habbaniya, how dangerous could it be?

4

The buildings at RAF Habbaniya were familiar. Classic 1930s British military. He could have been back at Chivenor.

But the daytime heat, followed by the night-time plunge into cold, gave away the fact he was no longer in England. That, and the shabby prefabricated structures just outside the inner gates.

By the time he reached the barrier that marked the inner camp, the breeze was rattling an RAF Ensign, high above him. Metal clips on the rope clanged against the pole.

A security checkpoint in the middle of an RAF station, something he'd never seen in England.

The barrier was down. Beyond it, the tarmac road became a dust track leading to a densely packed area of single-storey structures. Less sturdy and much less tidy than the rest of the station.

To the west, he could see the open area of taxiways and runway. Beyond that, an orange haze obscured the horizon.

"Dust is coming, sir."

Rob whipped around to find a small, rotund man

standing next to him, presumably having emerged from the guard hut.

He wore the same uniform as Asu: khaki drill with that slanted hat again, reminded him of the Anzacs. One side of the wide brim turned up.

The man was local. Dark skin and thick black moustache.

Epaulettes indicated his junior NCO rank, though Rob had no idea to what service he belonged.

"Hello, Corporal."

The man saluted; Rob returned the compliment.

"Am I going in the right direction for Cheapside?"

The corporal hesitated and glanced away. "Yes, sir. But best not to go at this time of day."

"It's rather important. You see, I need a tailor. Urgently."

As he said the words, he realised how silly they sounded.

Who needs an urgent tailor?

"Yes, please, sir. But maybe it's better to be there in the morning."

Rob shook his head. "That's too late. Is it that way?" He pointed ahead.

"About half a mile, sir." The corporal looked back towards his hut. "Please wait, please, sir." He disappeared into the sentry building and emerged a moment later with another man in a similar uniform, also with corporal stripes. "I will come with you. Seni at your service, sir." He turned to his colleague. "Abdullah, open the gate."

Rob looked back at the collection of huts. He was an RAF officer on an RAF station. How much danger could he be in? On the other hand, it would seem reckless not to accept the offer of an escort.

"Very well, but please, we must hurry."

Abdullah opened the gate to let them through before closing it with a clank behind them.

They reached the first intersection. The air took on a brown tint, a mix of the setting sun and a gathering dust storm.

"Down here." Seni led them along an avenue that ran at forty-five degrees from the crossroads. As they reached another junction, Rob noticed a small crowd of men, some sitting, around a doorway. They looked shabby and unshaven.

As Seni hurried them past, two of the men stepped out, not quite blocking their path. Seni seemed to deliberately shoulder-barge one, rather than step around him.

Rob looked back nervously. "Who are they?"

"Bad men. Iraqis."

Rob had to hold his hand in front of his face to protect his eyes from the growing barrage of airborne sand.

"What are you, then? If you don't mind my asking?"

Seni stopped and stood straight. "Levies, sir. The British Levies. Five years, sir. Like my father before me."

"I see," Rob said, barely understanding anything the man said. "Shall we carry on?"

"We are here, sir."

Rob looked over Seni's shoulder to see a wooden-framed shop front. In the window was a row of RAF desert drill shirts and jackets. It looked closed.

Next door was a similar display, with mess jackets of various sizes. Rob moved towards the second shop.

He banged on the door, struggling to make his knocking heard over the wind.

As he waited, he looked back down the street to see the group from the doorway drifting towards them.

"Dammit, open up," he said with a hiss under his breath.

"Please, sir. Best to come tomorrow," Seni said, as he cast a nervous glance at the approaching group.

"We must go now," the Assyrian said while staring past Rob.

He swivelled around to see two moustachioed policemen in Iraqi uniforms at the opposite end of the road.

"Police? That's good, isn't it? We'll be safe?"

"Please, sir. No. It is not good."

Rob looked between the shop and the group of men. The place was closed. The trip had been a dangerous waste of time.

"*Dammit.*"

They retraced their steps, back towards the crowd of men.

For the first time, Rob noticed a couple of them were carrying long, thin sticks.

As they got near, a man at the front of the group shouted something in Arabic. It didn't sound friendly.

Seni straightened his back and shouted, waving his hands in a gesture that seemed to say move aside.

The young men stood their ground.

Rob and Seni arrived in front of them. Rob looked back to see the policemen watching, maybe fifty yards back.

Seni shouted again; something in Arabic. Rob assumed it meant *get the hell out of our way.*

"Listen here. There's no need for any trouble," Rob said.

Seni pushed his way forward and again shoulder-barged the leader of the group. The man stumbled back, but a parting of the crowd allowed them to slip through. Seni paused and waved Rob ahead of him.

As Rob passed the last of the group, he heard a thump and turned around to see Seni sprawled on the ground.

He immediately bent down to help him but felt a shove in his side as the crowd closed around the downed man.

One of the group aimed a kick square at Seni's head.

"No!" Rob shouted.

But the group set upon Seni, kicking and punching. Rob grabbed a fistful of one man's loose robe and yanked him back. The man stumbled away from the group, and Rob looked in to see Seni cowering, arms clenched around his head as kicks continued to his body.

One man raised a stick.

"Stop! That's an order!" Rob shouted.

No one paid him any attention.

The stick came down on Seni's back, and he convulsed with pain.

A shoulder barge sent Rob tumbling behind the group.

As he hit the ground, he heard the unmistakable sound of a gunshot.

Instinctively, he covered his head with his arms and curled up.

In the darkness of his foetal position, he sensed the mood around him change.

The beating had stopped.

Was Seni dead?

Slowly, Rob moved his arms down and looked up to see a pot-bellied policeman looking down at him, pistol loosely held in his hand, a cigarette hanging from his mouth.

"Get up," the man said with a growl.

Slowly, Rob clambered to his feet, brushing the dust and sand from his uniform.

He heard a groan and looked down to see Seni, rolling onto his back. The side of his face was streaked with blood and desert.

Another policeman shouted something in Arabic at the attacking group.

The leader stepped forward. Immediately, the policeman landed a heavy punch to the man's jaw, sending him toppling backwards. The other men backed away.

The policeman turned to Rob, who also took a step back.

"This is no place for you. You belong in there. For now, at least. Stay inside the fence, for your protection."

Seni moaned beneath him, and Rob leant down to help him up.

"Please, sir. I am fine." He got to his feet and straightened his uniform. Blood ran down from his face. Buttons were missing from the top of his shirt; he did his best to pull it together before bending down to collect his crumpled and filthy hat, brushing it with his hand and placing it carefully back on his head.

The policemen offered no help.

"Go. And take your lapdog with you," the pot-bellied officer said, growling at Rob. "Your time in my country is at an end. You are no longer welcome."

Rob stared back at the policeman. What was he supposed to say? Was it his job to defend the treaty that allowed the RAF to operate from Habbaniya? Should he stand up for his uniform? For his Queen and Country?

He said nothing and turned to Seni.

"Are you sure you're all right? You're able to walk back with me?"

"Yes, sir."

The policeman took a step towards them.

"I think we'd better leave, then," Rob said.

He held out a hand to help Seni with his first few steps.

Some men around them sniggered.

Seni gradually became more upright, clearly trying to leave the scene with his head held high.

The blood was still pumping for Rob; his hands were shaking.

He'd never seen someone beaten up in his life. Just the odd, ineffective fight at school. Arms flailing, punches thrown that rarely found their mark.

But this was different.

Never kick a man when he's down, his father once told him.

The rules didn't apply here.

He suddenly felt a long way from home.

His mother told him he'd be homesick. He'd laughed it off, but she was right.

"Are you sure you're okay?" He asked Seni as they trudged back to the gate.

"Yes. You are kind to ask, sir. It is my sworn duty to protect you."

Seni was limping, the blood on his face and shirt drying quickly in the wind. Both men raised their hands to shelter their faces from the growing howl of the sandstorm.

"Who were they? Why did they attack you?" Rob had to raise his voice over the noise.

"They are bad people. Iraqis."

Rob shook his head, more confused than before.

They arrived back at the barrier. Safety.

Abdullah looked angry at the sight of Seni's face. He shouted a series of angry sentences. Seni waved him away and ushered Rob back onto the inner RAF station.

"Thank you, Seni. And I'm sorry for what happened to you."

Seni stood straight. He was dishevelled and bloodied, with a lopsided, out-of-shape hat. He took half a step backwards, brought his feet together, and presented Rob with a crisp salute.

It was both a pathetic and stirring sight.

Rob nodded at this obedient servant of the British, honoured to take a beating in the course of his duties.

Sand swirled around as Rob turned to leave.

The wind howl became a strange roar. Confused, he looked up in time to see a World War Two fighter—a Hawker Fury—sweep overhead, just a hundred feet above the ground.

"Please, sir. Prince Nuri," Seni shouted from behind him.

"That's him, flying?"

"Please, yes. Sir."

Rob watched the aircraft break through the circuit, disappearing into the limited visibility.

"In this storm? I hope he's a good pilot."

"Oh, sir. Prince Nuri is the best."

5

———————

"Prince Nuri is a bloody awful pilot."

Bunny spoke so quietly, Rob had to edge into the darkness of his room and lean forward to hear him.

His flight commander was sitting on his bed, head bowed, lit only by the light Rob had let in by opening his mess room door.

He had knocked twice before finally hearing the faintest "yes" from within.

Bunny's only reaction to Rob's tale of what happened on his trip to Cheapside was to disparage Prince Nuri.

Rob stood in the dark, unsure of what to do. A grown man he barely knew sat before him, hardly able to respond to normal conversation.

Had he received some bad news?

"Is everything all right, Bunny?"

His flight commander didn't respond.

Bunny's skin looked pale in the weak light. Dark patches under his eyes swallowed what little light made it to his face.

He looked like an old man on a park bench, running out

his life clock, feeding the ducks, not a fighter pilot still in his thirties.

"Shall I come back?" Rob asked.

Still nothing.

He backed out of the room.

"Sorry, chap," Bunny said, barely audible. "Mood dipped a bit."

His hands were clasped together on his lap, tightly entwined. And he was slightly rocking.

A shadow fell across the bed. Rob turned to see Asu in the doorway, holding a black bow tie and cummerbund.

"Oh, thank you, Asu. You've saved my life."

As Rob approached, Asu took a step back onto the covered walkway that ran alongside the single-storey mess building. He ushered Rob from the room and quickly closed the door behind him, leaving Bunny in the dark.

"Is Flight Lieutenant Pater-Smith okay, Asu?"

"Yes, sir. He is very well," Asu said quickly. "Sir, I think you have one hour until you are required in the anteroom. Malkuno has ironed your dress shirt."

Rob hesitated. He wanted to ask him more about Bunny, but he sensed further inquiry was not appropriate.

"Did you say Malkuno?"

"Sir, he is to be your batman. I have arranged it."

"I see, thank you." Rob turned to leave, as Asu moved towards Bunny's door.

"Asu?"

The batman turned to face him.

"Can I ask you a question?"

Asu glanced at the door and looked back at Rob with a hint of fear in his eyes.

Rob shook his head. "Not about Bunny."

Asu relaxed.

"I wanted to ask about the uniform you wear and the men at the gates. What is it?"

"The British Levies, sir."

Rob shook his head, trying to recall everything he'd learned about the British military. Nothing came to mind about any "Levies." "I'm sorry. Can you explain a bit more? Are you part of the British Army, like the Gurkhas?"

"I do not know who the Gurkhas are," Asu replied. He stood up straight. "We are Assyrians, sir."

"Assyrians?"

"Yes, sir. If you please, I will tell you we have lived here for very many years, but when Iraq was made by the British, we were not given our own land."

"I see. So you're Iraqi now?"

"No, sir. They do not like us. We commit a crime against them."

"A crime?"

"We are Christians, sir."

Rob scratched his chin. "And that's a crime? In 1957? They will arrest you for that?"

"We serve the British at Habbaniya, as the British Levies, sir. That is our protection."

6

An hour later, Rob swore for the eleventh time as he tried to fasten his bow tie. It was one of the many things he'd been taught as a pilot officer, but, unlike recovering from a spin, it continued to elude him.

He wanted Bunny's help, but the image of the lifeless man in the dark haunted him. He'd never seen anyone like that before.

He looked at his watch. One minute to seven.

"Shit."

He took a deep breath and held both ends of the tie.

There was a sharp rap at the door. Rob opened it to find Bunny with two glasses of something in his hands.

"A pre-drink before pre-drinks. What say you?"

Rob looked carefully at his flight commander. The bags under his eyes were still dark and sunken, the eyes puffy and red.

"I'd better stay clear headed for the check tomorrow," Rob said, looking suspiciously at the glass Bunny proffered.

"Nonsense. We drink and we fly. That's the Royal Air Force way. Should be our motto in Latin."

Rob stared for a second. This was the same man he'd seen in the depths of despair an hour ago?

He took a glass and sniffed it.

"Come on, May. It's just a G and T. I keep a little stash in the room. Never know when you need a livener."

He took a sip. Bunny pushed into Rob's room and looked around the place.

"I hear Asu has arranged your new batman. That's good. I can see he's keeping things in order."

"Um, yes. I haven't seen him yet, but my shirt was pressed."

Bunny's eyes went to the unfastened bow tie hanging from Rob's collar.

"Having difficulty, chap?"

"A little."

"Come on." He moved behind Rob, reaching over and picking up the two ends.

"I can only do it this way. Just like my mother did for me."

Rob winced at Bunny's breath on his neck, but his hands moved deftly to create an acceptable knot.

"Thank you," Rob said, as Bunny finished and took a seat in Rob's desk chair, the only one in the room. Rob checked the tie in the wardrobe mirror, with satisfaction.

Bunny's third distinct mood of the day was by far his best. Maybe a good time to discuss the dual check flight.

Rob pondered their postflight debrief. Something that bore no resemblance to the thorough discussions after most of his training sorties.

Go in with something personal.

"So, you're not married?" Rob asked, trying to sound casual while still looking in the mirror.

"And best off for it. Married to the Royal Air Force, old boy. She's my whore."

Rob turned to face him and summoned some courage.

"I genuinely thought we were too low and too fast. I thought it was a test, and that you were waiting for me to intervene."

Bunny took a long slug of his gin and tonic and smacked his lips as he placed the glass down. "You thought wrong." He sighed. "You're hesitant. I felt it in your first moves. I'll get you to engage with the aircraft. Take hold of events." He stood up. "But don't worry about it tonight. We'll get it sorted tomorrow."

Rob had no idea what he meant. *Engage with the aircraft* was not an expression he'd heard in flying training.

There was another rap at the door.

"Come!" Bunny shouted.

Asu opened the door and stepped inside.

"Please, sir," he said, addressing Bunny, "you are required by the squadron leader after the speeches. All flight commanders."

"I see. Thank you, Asu."

The corporal closed the door behind him.

"What do you think that's about?" Rob asked.

"We're off. You can bank on it. Just look at the expressions on the Assyrians' faces. They don't miss a thing, and they're nervous."

"So, why did Asu allocate Malkuno to me tonight, then, if he knows we're leaving?"

Bunny made for the door. "It's important to them to be attached to an officer. Asu's running around like a blue-arsed fly, making sure as many of his men are teamed up as possible. Not that it will make a blind bit of difference. But I suppose he's trying, and that's the main thing. They think their odds of getting to Blighty go up if they have an officer."

Rob followed him out and locked his room behind him.

"Oh, and one more thing," Bunny said. "Asu spent an hour making sure the gate guard you got beaten up was treated. His name's Seni. I think you owe him something. Tobacco should do the trick."

"Yes, Bunny."

Seni's smart salute in bloodied clothes flashed into his mind.

"Don't be an arse, May. Nobody cares about you, but having a tribesman slaughtered on your behalf is frowned upon."

He turned on his heels and headed down the corridor.

7

T he noise from the anteroom grew louder as they walked around to the front of the building.

"I assume the prince landed his Hawker Fury," Rob said.

"Assume nothing, old boy. He's quite capable of killing himself. We'll see whether there's an empty chair at the top table."

Two white-coated waiters opened the double doors as they approached. The sound of a hundred officers laughing and drinking swept over them. The mood was happy, smiles all round as they pushed their way through. Bunny swooped on a passing tray of Champagne and handed a glass to Rob.

"Cheers," he said, clinking, then downing half.

Rob looked across the crowd of heads. One man stood out. Tall, with the standard Middle Eastern moustache, a blue sash over his shoulder. He was smiling and chatting with the most senior officers.

"Ah, our erstwhile prince," Bunny said. "Living and breathing. Look at him, dripping with ill-founded confidence and ill-gotten gains."

"Gains?" Rob asked.

"The family's extremely rich in a part of the world where a British pound will buy you a house. Doesn't happen by playing nicely, I can tell you. Still, he's not a bad sort, and quite fond of me, as it happens. Listen, May, I'm going to rescue him from tedium. Be a good boy and go and find some junior pilots to play with. You can regale them with tales of your high japes outside the fence."

Bunny headed off to the group surrounding the prince. Rob watched him brush past the station commander, who seemed displeased by Bunny's arrival. The prince, however, beamed at him, and the two men hugged.

"May!"

Rob swivelled to see Clive Nuffield.

"Come and join us. We're planning to be the disreputable table."

Nuffield followed his eyeline. "Don't get any ideas about meeting the prince. He won't be introduced to the likes of us."

"I see Bunny's friendly with him," Rob said, as they made their way to a group of squadron pilots.

"Yes, well, Bunny can pretend to be anyone's friend when it suits him." Nuffield leant in closer to Rob. "The thing you have to remember about Bunny is that he's a spectacular cunt."

As soon as they sat down to dinner, the wine flowed. Waiters bustled around, ensuring the officers' glasses were always full.

"May, is it?" a pilot with several medals called from across the table.

"Yes."

"The new boy! Another JP to make me coffee. Brian Tilbert. You can call me Tilly."

"Hello, Tilly."

"Watch me carefully. I'm the best pilot on two-one-seven."

The other men at the table erupted into protest boos.

"Check the practice camp scores, boys. Check the scores."

"The weather clagged in for the rest of us in Cyprus, remember?" Nuffield said. "You were just lucky to get the first run."

Tilly shook his head and raised his glass. "If Peter May snicks one through the slips on his way to a century, it just says *century* in the book, doesn't it?" He turned back to Rob and tapped his nose. "It's the result that counts."

Rob laughed.

"What do you think of the Venom? Quite a beast, isn't she?" Tilly asked.

"Oh, erm, I haven't—"

"May'll be checked out tomorrow," Nuffield said quickly. "He'll get his hands on the Venom after that." He turned and winked at Rob.

The other pilot nodded slowly. "I thought you went up with Buns today?"

"And he wants another familiarisation flight with an experienced pilot," Nuffield said. "Something against that, Tilly?"

Tilly shrugged. "Fine. But don't dilly-dally. We're a couple of men short as it is. And you're going to love the Venom. Like a bloody Ferrari, she is." He took a swig of his Chablis and waved his glass in the air, moustache glistening. "As long as you treat her right, of course." He set the wine down and fixed Rob with an intense stare. "Have you read the notes? Ready for her?"

"I think so."

"After take-off checks!" he shouted.

Rob looked over his shoulder, then back at Tilly. "You want me to recite the checklist?"

"Come on, come on. You need to know these by heart. After take-off checks!"

"Not now, Tilly. We're trying to enjoy ourselves," Nuffield said.

"He needs to know these things, Nuff. Don't want to lose him on day one, do we?"

Rob closed his eyes. "For the Venom? Nose wheel up at eighty knots. Don't over-rotate. Dab the wheel brakes, select undercarriage up, raise flaps."

"And?" Tilly said.

Rob opened his eyes. The other pilots were watching him. This friendly banter had turned into an *ad hoc* assessment.

"Oh, switch on hood seal and cockpit pressure."

Tilly narrowed his eyes and studied Rob. "Good. Don't forget. If you climb without pressure, you could black out before you realise something's up. Silly way to meet your maker."

"Right, yes." Rob nodded. He was about to finish his glass of wine, but hesitated.

Nuffield leant over. "Oxygen will sort out your hangover. Couple of deep breaths when you strap in, and you'll be right as rain."

He downed the last of the red. As his empty glass landed on the table, a waiter appeared and refilled it.

The others around the table got into their own conversations. Rob leant towards Nuffield.

"Can I ask you more about Bunny?"

Nuffield raised his eyebrows. "What do you want to know?"

"He was . . . odd this evening. I found him sat on his bed, in the dark."

Nuffield nodded. "Yes, he'll do that. Just ignore him. He comes back to life."

Someone called Nuffield's name, and he switched his attention across the table.

Food arrived. More drinks. The noise level rose.

As the waiters cleared away the sticky toffee pudding, the station commander rose to his feet.

A hush descended.

"Mr Vice? The loyal toast."

A flying officer from another squadron stood and held up a glass. The room rose with him.

Rob wobbled as he stood up, perhaps a little too quickly after downing most of a bottle of wine.

"The Queen!" the junior officer shouted.

"THE QUEEN!" the room roared back with one voice.

"Gentlemen, you may now smoke." The CO sat back down.

"No speeches?" one man asked.

"Not so lucky," Tilly said, looking across to the top table as the CO took to his feet again.

"Gentlemen, today it is my sad duty to inform you we are leaving."

The room erupted.

Jeers, boos, howls of protest.

The CO put up both hands to quell the crowd.

"You know that things have become sticky for the United Kingdom in Iraq of late. We have tried earnestly to extend or renew our treaty. However, it is not to be, and the leaders in Iraq have let us know they expect us to leave forthwith.

"I, for one, feel we should applaud their sense of independence. Let us taint our sadness with pride that a young country wishes to break out from its former guardians."

The crowd muttered and grumbled, clearly unconvinced by this optimistic view of what was happening in the country.

"We built this airfield in 1934. Nearly a quarter of a century later, we can look back on our contribution to Iraq with pride. We have employed many thousands of locals. And of course we have supported, and in turn been supported by, a large number of the Iraqi Assyrian population, who proudly serve in the British Levies. We have provided work, accommodation, and status to a people who in turn have proved to be Her Majesty's most loyal servants."

Applause started; officers raised their hands to clap the few Assyrians in the room, mainly waiting staff who stood at the back.

Nuffield leant over to Rob. "They're going to need more than a bloody round of applause."

The CO continued.

"But the world does not stand still, and we must react to the situation. We leave with our heads held high. It is my firm belief, backed by our record keeping, that Royal Air Force Habbaniya has been the finest, most active, and most deadly of Her Majesty's stations beyond the United Kingdom's shores."

The room cheered.

"Lately, we have been honoured by the patronage of Prince Nuri of the Iraqi royal family. And he has requested this opportunity to address you all." The CO turned to his guest. "Your Highness."

Nuri rose to his feet and surveyed the room. Under his blue sash was an Iraqi air force uniform, adorned with pilots wings and enough gold braid to make a set of curtains.

The room fell silent as the prince's gaze slowly swept left to right.

"Playing to the gallery?" Tilly whispered.

"I wish to lay my eyes upon this glorious sight one last time. The finest air force in the world, and the finest squadrons in that air force. And with the Venom, the finest fighter jet!" The room laughed politely.

"Better not tell him about the Javelin," Tilly said in a low voice.

"Although, sadly, you never allowed me to fly one," Nuri said, turning back to the CO, who smiled.

"You've got your own," the station commander quipped.

"Ah, but it's the Iraqi Air Force, not the Royal Iraqi Air Force. You're not the only ones for whom doors are now closing."

The top table nodded in agreement.

"As you can see, the times are changing. I hope you will allow me to speak my mind, without causing any undue offence. My brother, the King, may be content to be swept along by events. I am content only to shape those events. It is my belief that we, the true Iraqi leaders, must take the action we need to preserve our status. I am not foolish. I know there are men in our armed forces who would see my brother hanging from a lamp-post in Baghdad. And me, for that matter. But there are those who are loyal to the Crown among them. My brother will take no action, but I will ensure when the time comes, we are not outnumbered. Sadly, it is no longer the case that I will be able to rely on my good friends at Royal Air Force Habbaniya. But with the bravery I have learned from you, I will fight for what I believe, just like Mr Churchill. So, it is with a heavy heart and reluctance I bid you farewell. Let us hope we meet again. Maybe there will be a time soon, when you will be welcomed back by a stronger royal family." He clasped his hands together. "Thank you, friends, thank you."

His voice broke with the last sentence, and he sat down to a warm round of applause that quickly became a standing ovation. There was even some cheering.

"God, is he crying?" someone at Rob's table asked.

The applause continued. A chant began.

"Habbaniya! Habbaniya!"

There was a palpable weight in the room, the realisation this was a key moment in British history.

The last supper of RAF Habbaniya.

Like all trainee officers, Rob had heard tales of wild dining-in nights on the squadrons. It felt likely he was about to experience one for himself.

Nuffield leant across to him as they both continued clapping. "This is going to be messy."

No one resumed his seat. Instead, the men wrestled their way to the bar, where the noise level had now ramped up several decibels.

The chatter focused on the CO's words. He'd made it sound as if they were to leave right away. When? Tomorrow?

No one seemed to know, but Rob noticed Bunny, Nuffield, and Tilly fall in with Squadron Leader Forsythe, the 217 boss. The group exited the room with the senior men from the other squadrons.

Left to their own devices, the junior officers began drinking more heavily than usual. And it was usual to drink extremely heavily.

It wasn't long before the first empty can of Stella Artois

hit the ceiling fan. It pinged off the whirring blades and struck an unfortunate officer in the forehead.

Rob and a few others helped as the man recovered his composure on the floor, a bright red bloodstain on his pristine white shirt.

Rob stood up to see the squadron hierarchies had returned.

Bunny was in deep conversation with Prince Nuri.

The injured officer stumbled to his feet. He put up a finger as if to make an announcement. A relative hush fell around him.

"Brigadoon!" he shouted. This drew an enormous cheer. Immediately, the room filled with the sound of furniture scraping across the floor as the men cleared a space.

Nuffield laid a hand on Rob's shoulder.

Rob frowned. "What's going on?"

"We're playing Brigadoon. And you're the most junior pilot on the station. Come this way."

Rob followed Nuffield to the fireplace, where an enthusiastic fire party prepared a small cannon.

"Oh, God," Rob said, and watched as a tennis ball was loaded into a plastic tube as a small banger was inserted into the other end.

Nuffield thrust a can of beer into his hand.

"Hold this high over your head," Nuffield said, placing him ten yards from the cannon.

"Then what?" Rob asked.

"Pray."

8

A sharp knocking sound shifted Rob from a deep slumber.

He groaned and shifted onto his side, hesitantly opening his eyes.

A white blob resolved into his mess kit piled unceremoniously on the floor.

His head was full of wool; his ears rang.

He hauled himself up and opened the door to find a staring Malkuno.

"Do I look that bad?"

Malkuno quickly regained his composure and stood up straight.

"No, sir. Not at all."

Malkuno loitered. Even hungover, or possibly still drunk, Rob knew this was an awkward situation.

"Look, I think we're all leaving, so I don't see the need for you to start . . ."

Malkuno's face crumpled. His body wilted, and his head bowed. He nodded and looked back at Rob with moist eyes. "Yes, sir."

Bunny's words came back to Rob: how important it was to the batmen to be attached to an officer.

In the dim light of the officers' mess accommodation corridor, Rob saw first-hand how much it meant.

"But of course, if you'd like to . . . ?"

Malkuno snapped his heels together and saluted. "It would be my most sincere honour."

Rob nodded slowly and turned to look back at his room.

"I'm sorry it's a bit of a mess, but if you wouldn't mind . . ." He trailed off as Malkuno swept past him and gathered his strewn kit. Scooping up the debris, he trotted out, without saying another word.

Rob was left staring in the mirror, at the full extent of his black eye.

He put a hand to the swollen lid and immediately withdrew it as a sharp pain spread across the side of his face.

No wonder Malkuno had looked so shocked when he'd opened the door.

What must they think of us?

He slumped onto the bed, bitterly regretting the last ten beers.

His flying coverall hung on the wardrobe door. But with Habbaniya abandoned, would he need it again?

In theory, he had a second dual check with Bunny in the Vampire.

"Great," he said with a sigh.

BREAKFAST WAS BUSY AND LOUD. Officers barked cheery greetings as they passed one another. Rob wondered how he could be the only one to feel fatally hungover?

They're all pretending to be fine.

Clearly, it was not the done thing to show any form of drinking consequence.

"My God. What a shiner!" Nuffield appeared next to him.

"Thanks."

Rob took a seat next to Bunny on a long table with Tilly and various other 217 officers. Nuffield took a seat opposite and ordered coffee and breakfast for Rob and him.

Bunny looked up at him and shook his head without saying a thing.

"It's fine. Doesn't hurt." Rob shifted in his seat.

"Mess cannons have probably killed in the past," said Bunny. "So, perhaps count yourself lucky."

"So," a junior pilot a couple of seats down began saying. "What's happening? What's the drill for leaving?"

Bunny and Nuffield exchanged a quick look.

"You'll get the details after the weather brief," Bunny said.

"But come on, chaps. You know, right?"

Nuffield scratched his chin and shrugged. "It's not a secret. We're off. End of the month is the official deadline, but top brass is getting jumpy about the natives. They want the shiny stuff out right away. End of tomorrow at the latest."

"End of tomorrow?" the junior pilot said. "How? Where?"

"To Cyprus as a staging post," Nuffield said. "And Bunny is the logistics man, God help us."

Bunny finished a forkful of baked beans. "As you know, we're in the unusual position of having more aircraft than pilots. So we need to box clever. Ten of you lot will fly a Venom each to Akrotiri today. All junior pilots." He glanced at Rob. "Not you."

Rob's face flushed red. His failure to pass a simple dual check yesterday was now seriously hampering the operation to leave Habbaniya.

"That leaves five pilots for seven jets. So we need to shuttle two Venoms over the border to Amman. Two-one-three Squadron will take ownership. The station support Anson will leave here ahead of the transit to ferry the two pilots back. Which gives us five pilots and five Venoms for a dignified departure tomorrow. Last ones out, please turn off the lights."

Rob remained motionless as the group burst into an active discussion about the plan, speculating on who was doing what.

Bunny's words sounded sharp in his head.

Not you, May. What does that mean? *You've failed. You'll be sitting in the back row of a transport, along with the junior technicians?*

"By the way, Six Squadron have it a lot worse than us, logistically," Bunny said to the group. "But that's their problem. Do not under any circumstances volunteer to help them. We need all the men we can get." He stuffed the last of his sausage into his mouth and stood up.

A waiter appeared and placed a full English breakfast in front of Rob and Clive Nuffield.

"You haven't got time for breakfast, May," Bunny said sternly. "You're ferrying a Venom to Amman with me, as long as you can pass a bloody dual check."

9

The squadron offices were quiet, with most of the men still at breakfast.

As they'd left the mess, Bunny had told Rob to check out both of their sets of flying equipment while he sorted some final details.

Rob had to wait for a corporal to appear at the equipment hatch, but eventually, he emerged back into the office with arms laden. He dropped everything onto a map table without a helmet or life vest hitting the floor.

He looked up and out of the window.

Outside, Bunny had Asu by the collar, shouting into the man's face.

Rob looked around. Was anyone else seeing this? Apparently not.

As he watched, Bunny shoved Asu behind a shed on the edge of the hardstanding. Asu held up a solitary finger. He seemed to say no, and yet Bunny continued to manhandle him.

Just as they disappeared from view, Rob thought he saw Bunny raising an arm to strike his batman.

He stumbled backwards in shock, looking around.

Someone needed to protect Asu.

But the room was empty. He walked to the far end, where a corridor led to the equipment hatch, staffed by a corporal. There might be an officer there.

"Right! Let's commit aviation!" came a loud call from behind.

Rob stopped and turned to see Bunny picking up his helmet and oxygen mask.

He marched towards the door.

"Come on, May. You've got a dual check to pass."

As Bunny pushed through the door, Rob glimpsed Asu hurrying towards the hangar.

He disappeared into the gloom of the large building.

10

R ob arrived at the Vampire and dropped his kit on the ground next to the fuselage. He looked up at Bunny, who had begun to dress for the flight. He was humming to himself.

"Is everything all right, Bunny?"

Bunny looked up and appeared surprised.

"Yes! Why shouldn't it be? Come on, come on. We need to get this done."

Slowly, Rob began his walk-around of the two-seat fighter jet. As he reached the tail fin and checked the pitot tube, he resolved to put what he'd seen out of his mind, at least for now. He would speak to Asu when they got back.

He needed to concentrate on the flight.

If he failed, all the plans they'd drawn up would be in jeopardy.

His stomach prickled with nerves.

As he reached the left-hand side of the cockpit, Bunny was already strapping into the right-hand seat.

He finished his walk-around, donned his flying clothing,

and climbed in, tightening his straps, pressed arm-to-arm with his eccentric flight commander.

Bunny spoke without looking up. "Yesterday, your steep turn was eighty-five degrees, not ninety. You failed to restart the heading indicator between dynamic manoeuvres, and you rejoined at seven hundred seventy-five feet, not eight hundred." He looked up. "I don't care that you grabbed the controls, but you need to fly accurately. Understood?"

Rob nodded.

With his local area chart tucked beside his seat, Rob opened the checklist. It got caught on the ring binder, and he struggled for a moment to get it to open fully.

"Bloody thing," he muttered in frustration.

Bunny reached over and pushed the pad down into his lap. "Breathe," he said. "Take your time. Ask if you're not sure. Show me the decision-making."

Rob tried to move more deliberately. He reached forward and neutralised the dials in order before continuing through the checks.

Five minutes later, he acknowledged the sight of two chocks held up by a marshaller standing to the side of the jet and edged the throttle forward. The Goblin engine whined a little louder, and the Vampire shifted from its moorings.

Once in the air, Bunny put him through his paces. But unlike the day before, this trip was significantly more sedate. His flight commander calmly asked for a demonstration of handling in measured sequences. He was a different person from the day before.

Rob's eyes moved from the airspeed indicator to the artificial horizon, and outside to the actual horizon, which was a hazy white in the morning sun.

He was getting used to the indistinct desert horizon, and

he worked as hard as he ever had in an aircraft to hit the numbers as precisely as possible.

When he overshot his rollout onto a southerly heading, he quickly put in opposite control and snagged one hundred eighty degrees exactly.

"Good," Bunny said.

After fifteen more minutes of general handling, Bunny ordered him to rejoin.

Carefully, Rob made his radio calls and descended the aircraft to eight hundred feet.

He recalled one of the stricter instructors earlier in his training, always shouting something such as "I didn't ask you to fly seven hundred ninety-eight feet, May."

But the altimeter wasn't that accurate; for a start, the white needle covered about twenty feet on the dial. But the principle was there. Fly the numbers precisely. Keep your margins healthy, for the time it goes wrong.

He rolled the Vampire onto a downwind leg, calling final as he banked in a smooth arc onto the centre line of Habbaniya's main runway.

The Vampire wheels touched down with a satisfying clunk. Rob hesitated before braking, fully expecting a touch-and-go to be ordered by Bunny.

"Full stop, May. Taxi back."

He did as he was told.

The taxi continued in silence. Rob reached for his checklist and completed the shutdown.

Bunny looked out the canopy to the right, humming.

As Rob lifted the small lever that released the canopy and let fresh air back in, Bunny lifted himself out of the cramped space, groaning as he did so.

Rob stared after him as his flight commander hurried away from the aircraft.

. . .

HE CAUGHT up with Bunny as they approached the squadron building.

"Be a good sort. Look after this." Bunny said, handing Rob his flying kit.

Rob, juggled two helmets and life vests. "You don't want Asu to take it?"

"Oh, he's off on a jaunt. Some secret Assyrian business, no doubt."

Rob balanced his load of flying helmets, oxygen masks, and life jackets. Bunny headed off away from the building.

"So . . . I've passed the dual check?" Rob shouted after him.

Bunny stared back at him. "Of course. How the fuck else do we get the squadron out of here? Now, be a good boy and plan our run to Amman. Stick to the supply route via Trebil. Got it?"

"Supply route, via Trebil," Rob repeated as if it were an air traffic instruction. But Bunny was gone, disappearing around the corner of the hangar.

11

The offices of 217 Squadron were busy, as dozens of men worked on taking down and packing the vast amount of paperwork and stores.

They ushered the full boxes outside into a trailer, which they attached to a tractor.

Rob dropped both his and Bunny's flying equipment on a spare desk and quickly pushed himself against it, as two more boxes were hustled out by a short corporal, just about peering over them.

Out of the window, the tractor driver jumped on and drove the full trailer to the centre of the apron, parking in front of the neat line of Venoms.

Rob furrowed his brow. Surely they couldn't put the boxes in a small fighter? Was there some strange carrying capacity? Perhaps an empty fuel tank . . .

Out of the corner of his eye, he saw the huge nose of a transport aircraft emerge like a whale from beyond the control tower.

In grey with flashes of orange and black, the distinctive shape of a Blackburn Beverley crossed the apron and came to a halt in front of a small team of marshallers. It parked fifty yards from the Venoms, before two of the engines on one side powered up and spun her around, facing back out to the airfield.

Even inside the building, the noise was loud enough for men to pause their packing and look out.

"She's here!" one of the senior officers announced. "Let's get in first before Six Squadron nab all the space."

The rate of industry went up a notch.

Rob turned his attention to his after-flight paperwork, filling in both his and Bunny's flying logs.

"*May!*"

Nuffield loomed over him.

"Hello, Clive."

"Let me guess? Bunny Pater-Smith left you to do the legwork on your jaunt to Amman?"

"Yes."

"Follow me."

Nuffield led him to a side room with maps pinned to the walls. He ran his hand along the easterly line from Habbaniya to Jordan.

"As you can see, once you're east of Ramadi, there's naff all along the route. There used to be a radio bearing available from Amman, but it's been off for a while now. So use dead reckoning and regular waypoints, but choose them with care. It all looks the same out there, and nav can be tricky. You wouldn't be the first to wander hundreds of miles off course."

Rob gazed at the featureless desert stretching out to the Jordanian border and beyond.

"Bunny told me to follow the supply route." He squinted at the map. "And cross at Trebil." He pointed to a small border town.

Nuffield put his spectacles on and peered at the chart. "Whatever he wants, I suppose. Badlands around Trebil, though. Don't have an engine failure. We won't get to you before the brigands do, and one of Her Majesty's de Havilland Venoms will become a chicken coop for the rest of its life." He laughed.

"Right," Rob said, scratching his chin. This was actual responsibility, not pretending to be in charge with an instructor watching over. He was actually in charge of a sortie that needed to be planned and executed meticulously.

Nuffield fished a scrawl-covered notepad out of his pocket. Every inch was covered by planning notes and scribblings. The man was busy. Nuffield flipped through the pages and located what he was looking for. "The Anson left at oh nine forty-five, so will be there plenty ahead of you. Hopefully, the crew won't be too drunk to fly you back. And a chap called Swift from two-one-three squadron will be on the ground to take possession of the Venoms. It'll be quiet when you get back. Just us execs and you. The chosen one." He frowned at Rob. "You must have made quite an impression on Bunny. That, or he wants something from you. Anyway, you can look forward to one final night of debauchery after thirty glorious years in Habbaniya."

Rob was still feeling the effects of alcohol and the mess-cannon shot he took to the eye, and he couldn't countenance the idea of another night, even if it was just half a dozen officers.

Instead, he squinted at the chart, looking for a scale.

"It's about four fifty to Amman," Nuffield said. "It'll be a slow haul back in the Anson, of course." He looked at his watch. "So, I'd leave sooner rather than later." Nuffield made for the door. "Oh, and don't forget what I said about choosing waypoints carefully. No room for cock-ups today."

Rob fished a clean chart out of a brown paper wallet. "I'll have Bunny with me, won't I?"

Nuffield let out a laugh as he left.

Alone in the room, Rob opened the chart and laid it out on a large map table.

He pulled out a china pencil and marked it up.

Nuffield wasn't exaggerating about the lack of features. Once the highway ran out, it was all dirt tracks and small settlements. Only a few seemed to be named on the map.

He spotted a series of marks in the ground—probably water treatment or reservoir pens—and used them to mark the first waypoint past Ramadi.

He continued to find what he could, to use as navigation fixes until eventually drawing the final line into Amman airfield.

The Jordanian city stood out with its dense colours of urbanisation. And typically for an old town, it was built on a confluence of rivers.

He ran his finger along the route he'd chosen, carefully looking either side of the line for any airspace they needed to avoid. But unlike the UK's crowded traffic lanes, the chart showed an empty sky, like the land beneath it.

He then set about marking transit altitudes, referring to the Venom pilot's notes for optimal fuel burn conditions. He was pleased to note the range of the twin-tailed fighter was twice what they would need.

After he annotated the chart with the right frequencies, Rob took a step back and surveyed his work.

Again, he felt a shudder of significance. This was the real thing. Even though the instructors left you alone towards the end of training, you couldn't escape the fact that they were still there, in the background, and ultimately they wouldn't knowingly allow you to fly into an unsafe position.

But here it was all up to him.

Nuffield's laugh echoed in his mind. No Bunny for back-up.

If Rob got the fuel calculations wrong, it seemed unlikely Bunny would notice, anyway. He took such little interest in the details. Rob imagined the engines flaming-out over the middle of the desert and, in the event they survived, being hauled up in front of a court martial.

He went into the main office to get the latest weather, then returned to go over every heading and leg again, updating the durations and recalculating the fuel burn.

He suddenly missed his friends from Chiv. Even on solo tasks, they checked each other's work, sharing the burdens and talking everything through.

He could ask Nuffield to double-check his planning, but the man had a million things to organise.

The weather was clear, apart from some fairly strong surface winds, not untypical for the desert.

He turned as the door opened with a *whoosh*.

"It's always sunny in the Middle East," Bunny announced, looking over his shoulder.

"Yes, it's fine. I've finished the route."

"Oh, right. Good-oh." Bunny studied his watch. "No rush. Shall we say fifteen hundred for the departure?"

Bunny headed out, not waiting for an answer.

12

R ob found himself alone in the squadron over the lunch period. Time moving slowly. They were surely leaving it too late to set off on a thousand-mile round trip, returning in a slow prop aircraft. Why wouldn't they plan to run in daylight?

He didn't want to go over Bunny's head, but he had an idea. Perhaps he should contrive to bump into Clive Nuffield in the mess, where he assumed the remaining members of the squadron were having lunch. Surely Nuff would want to know why they hadn't already left?

He walked back onto the main RAF station and along the straight that led to the mess annexe where the men dined.

He heard a petrol lawnmower somewhere in the distance. The grass on either side of the road was neatly trimmed. In the short time he'd been there, he'd seen a small army of Assyrian workers tending to every blade.

The area around the flag staff, the centre of the station, was immaculate. The way it had been for three decades.

Who will cut the grass tomorrow, he wondered.

Pushing the mess door open, it was immediately apparent Clive Nuffield was not there. In fact, the room contained only two members of staff clearing the last of the crockery. It must have been a very small turnout for lunch.

And where was Nuffield? No doubt sleeves rolled up, mired in more planning tasks, elsewhere on RAF Habbaniya.

Back in the squadron building, the wall clock ticked slowly around to 11:40. The clock had a large *Z* across its face, indicating it was set to Zulu: Greenwich Mean Time. It was actually 14:40 local time.

Finally, it was time to leave.

He gathered his and Bunny's flying gear and shuffled through the quieter planning room. The planning paperwork was tucked underneath his bundle of equipment.

The line of silver aircraft was getting shorter, with three formations already on the ground in Cyprus.

Mechanics climbed over four of the Venoms. There was no slack for them; each aircraft had to be airworthy for the evacuation.

Rob spotted the squadron boss, Wing Commander Roger Dearing, in conversation with a small team of engineers. He had deep worry lines etched across his face.

"Poor sods had to get every jet airworthy," Bunny said as he arrived alongside Rob. "Probably never been done before."

Rob handed him his flying equipment.

Bunny passed him a Browning 9 mm pistol in return.

"Really?"

Bunny shrugged. "Standard procedure, old boy. You never know. Now, which are our jets?" He looked down the line.

"Bravo and kilo," Rob said, looking at his notes. "I'm told they'll be at the end."

As they arrived at the two Venoms furthest from the buildings, a knot tightened in Rob's stomach. He'd rapidly progressed from a failed check in a Vampire to a single-seat high-performance fighter, on a one-way trip that wasn't allowed to go wrong.

"You've read the notes?"

"Sorry?"

"The notes, May! Have you memorised the boldface actions for the Venom?"

Rob nodded. Images of the emergency drills floated through his mind.

"Right. Get airborne. Do one circuit, then meet me. I'll be holding to the south."

"You want me to do a circuit? Do we have time?"

"We don't want your first-ever landing in a Venom to be at an international airport in Amman, do we? Have a quick practice here."

Bunny disappeared to the last Venom on the line, and Rob's eyes fell on what was to be his jet. The serial WR492 emblazoned on the side, with a name stencilled under the canopy: "Flt Lt R Cotton."

He pushed against a small panel near the printed squadron crest and released the canopy, sliding the hood back, and dropped his chart and helmet onto the seat before walking around.

He squinted into the air intakes tucked against the fuselage, eyes searching for debris or foreign objects. Birds had been known to make their homes in there overnight; a nest could destroy an engine on startup.

Rob was now singularly responsible for the finely balanced evacuation plan.

The feeling of dread solidified, like a cloud above him.

Despite the long wait, he now felt the planning he'd done was rushed.

Inexperience, he told himself. He wasn't senior enough for this level of responsibility. Damn Bunny for disappearing all day! He hadn't even checked the route.

He reached into the intake and felt all the way to the fan blades, just to be sure.

He performed the rest of the checks carefully, but as he got to the far side of the Venom, he heard a sudden whine and realised Bunny was already starting up.

He hurried around, making sure the pitot tube and static vent were clear of insects before donning his helmet and climbing in. A marshaller stood by as he went through the pre-start list.

Rising panic. Rob hated being rushed. During training, he made a habit of getting out early to the aircraft to give him time to settle.

He checked his straps, picked up his checklists, and rushed through the pre-start actions, eventually signalling to the marshaller, who moved a couple of yards back as Rob fired the cartridge.

The engine caught quickly, and before Rob could even signal again, the marshaller was heading back down the line of aircraft. No doubt there was much engine testing to be done that afternoon.

Rob looked to his right, but Bunny was gone.

He scanned the airfield ahead to see the twin-boom back-end of a Venom trundling at a fast taxi away from him.

Come on, come on. For Christ's sake.

Sweat formed on his brow.

Rob pulled the canopy shut and pressed the transmission switch.

He froze.

He couldn't remember his call sign.

Quickly looking down, he pushed the checklists to one side and found his briefing paper, then took a deep breath.

"Gauntlet One is ready for taxi, for one circuit and departure to the east. "

"Gauntlet One. Clear for taxi. Runway two three is active."

"Gauntlet One. Clear for taxi."

He looked up again to see Bunny's Venom had disappeared from view, presumably beyond the control tower.

Rob released the park brake, looked ahead, and moved the throttle forward.

The jet engine noise grew, and the vibration rose through his seat.

The aircraft lurched an inch forward, straining to continue.

But it didn't move.

Something was wrong.

He immediately snapped the throttle back to idle, and his eyes darted to the brake switch. Was it really off?

He cycled it and pulled his feet completely off the rudder pedals in case he had been inadvertently pressing on the individual wheel brakes.

"Are you joining me at some point?" Bunny shouted on the radio, clearly ignoring the etiquette.

"Gauntlet One. You are required to expedite your taxi, please. We have a transport on long final."

Confusion had set in. Rob's heart was thumping.

What the hell was wrong with this thing?

He tried again. The thrust increased, and the aircraft felt as if it were trying to move, but something was holding it back.

Air traffic gave Bunny permission to take-off and Rob

glanced up to see a cloud of black smoke trail from behind the accelerating fighter.

He brought his eyes back inside his cockpit, urgently searching the controls for a sign that one of them was in the wrong position.

"Goddamit, what's wrong?"

In his peripheral vision, he saw a marshaller running towards him. The man was pointing at his aircraft and shouting.

He snapped the throttle to idle again.

He had a sudden fear.

Am I on fire?

Rob whipped his head around to view the engine and rear of the aircraft. No sign of flames, just some black smoke from behind. Normal for the Venom.

The marshaller reached him and dived under the aircraft, emerging a moment later with two bright yellow chocks.

He walked away, shaking his head.

Rob had no idea whether it was his fault or the over-stretched ground crew's.

Probably his.

He moved the throttle again, and this time the Venom rolled away from its place at the end of the line as he taxied out to the active runway. The wheels of the Venom bounced over the tarmac, transmitting every bump and hollow to his backside.

As he rounded the last turn that led to the end of the runway, he squeezed the transmit button.

"Gauntlet One is ready for take-off."

"Hold at Alpha. Do not enter the active."

"Dammit." Rob punched the transmit button. *"Roger hold. Gauntlet One."*

The transport on final was too close to allow him to take off ahead.

A further delay.

He turned and scanned the approach. A silver Vickers Valetta, nose slightly raised, was descending about half a mile away.

Rob's fingers tapped on the control column as he waited for the twin-propellered aircraft to pass in front. It seemed to ride on the ground effect cushion forever, before finally settling down onto the Habbaniya runway.

"Gauntlet One, line up and wait."

"Line up and wait. Gauntlet One." Rob rolled the Venom onto the runway, quickly carrying out his final pre-take-off checks.

Ahead of him, the Valetta turned off, and Air Traffic gave him permission to leave.

The kick in his back from the engine surprised him, although he knew the Ghost jet engine had a significant power jump on the Goblin he was used to in the Vampire.

The jet quickly got to eighty knots, at which point he eased the stick back, but was careful not to nudge the tail onto the runway.

One of the many friendly warnings he'd received.

The Venom lifted gracefully into the air, and for a moment, Rob smiled.

He raised the landing gear. With the wheels out of the airstream, the aircraft accelerated even more quickly, and he tempered it by taking off an inch of throttle.

He allowed his Venom to climb to five hundred feet before rolling left into the circuit. His hands moved quickly across the controls to complete the after-take-off checks by losing the twenty degrees of flaps.

He called downwind, suddenly realising he was rapidly approaching the turn onto final.

Too fast.

He pulled the throttle back to idle and held the nose up, desperate to scrub off the excess speed. Glancing to his left, he saw the wing was level with the undershoot. It was already time to bank, and he hadn't run through his down-wind checks.

He simultaneously rolled the aircraft and ran through another memorised list of actions, saying them out loud.

"Air brakes IN. Undercarriage LEVER FULLY DOWN." He watched, willing the three green lights to show the gear was down and locked. A whirring mechanical noise sent vibrations into his seat.

"Come on, come on!"

He was going wide. The aircraft was lumbering with full internal tanks and full tip tanks on the ends of the wings.

He banked more steeply to bring it back, still willing the landing-gear lights to show.

Rob rolled onto a wonky short final, just seconds from touchdown, before the green lights finally flickered on.

He rattled through the final checks, long after the point he should have carried them out.

"Brakes, *Pressure off,* Flap *twenty.* Fuel high-pressure pump isolating switch *off.* Harness *tight and locked.* Hood Seal *off.*"

He was fast and high.

The airspeed showed one hundred twenty-three knots.

The heavy aircraft had momentum.

As the needle got down to one hundred ten, he eased the throttle forward, but he was already over the piano keys, and too high for the standard touchdown point.

The notes said not to let the Venom go below one

hundred five knots with a full fuel load. His eyes flashed between the ASI and the runway ahead.

So much to do in a fast-moving jet.

He was still high.

Pushing the nose down, he reduced power. The speed dropped to one hundred five.

"Bollocks!"

Brown desert surrounding the RAF airfield filled his side views.

Too steep, too slow.

Time to throw this landing away.

He shoved the throttle to full power and waited for the heavy jet to respond. It took a second, and the wheels grazed the runway, probably two hundred yards long from the intended touchdown point.

The Venom bounced back into the air, and he had to work the stick to keep the nose on the horizon.

It felt ragged, untidy.

Bunny's voice came over the radio. "I don't know what the hell that was, but it will have to do."

Rob was busy with his climb-out checks. He closed the hood vent as reminded at dinner; was that just last night?

"I need to try again," Rob said.

"No time. We press on. Let's go east, young man. Lead the way."

Rob made the radio call to Habbaniya tower, and let his airspeed rise to two hundred fifty knots before putting the Venom in a climb. They were to transit at thirty thousand feet.

He retrieved the chart from his side and looked at the first waypoint. He'd used the northern extent of Lake Habbaniya as an obvious geographical point to spot.

At least it was on the map.

Only now he was airborne and looking down at the actual ground, it was clear the lake had shrunk from the size on the charts.

The outline was still marked, though, by a change in the colour of the earth. He gave it his best guess and started the stopwatch as he passed overhead.

It occurred to him he hadn't formatted with Bunny.

He looked over his shoulder while calling the new heading and duration for the leg. "Zero nine eight for twelve minutes. Fourteen seconds at two fifty knots."

"Roger," Bunny said. He sounded calm enough. But what was the procedure? Should Rob confirm the formation is visual? That's what they'd done in training.

He caught a movement in his periphery and swivelled to see Bunny joining him in echelon right.

"Good afternoon! How are you finding her?"

"Erm. Nice."

It was all Rob could think to say. So far, the Venom had been quicker than he expected and had got away from him during his first attempted circuit. Which wasn't a great feeling.

The mass of dense homes and buildings grew to their left as they passed south of Ramadi.

Rob squinted, trying to pick out the royal palaces each Iraqi city seemed to possess. He imagined the opulence of Prince Nuri's life amid the abject poverty. Not something he'd thought much about before Bunny had mentioned it.

There was something admirable about the prince, though. He clearly thought a lot of the RAF, and had been genuinely moved by the news that Habbaniya was to be abandoned.

They reached their cruise altitude, and Rob made a note

to expect the next waypoint to be a few seconds late, thanks to the loss of ground speed during the climb.

He exhaled. Checking the aircraft was in trim, he took his hands off the controls and rested them on the sides of the canopy.

The Venom stayed true, straight, and level.

A pair of Royal Air Force Venoms, drawing a straight line across the Iraq landscape.

Rob looked behind Bunny's jet. After a gap of a hundred yards, a bright white contrail had formed. From the ground, it would look like two crisp lines across an empty blue sky. What would the tribesmen in the middle of nowhere make of it?

They made a last radio call to Habbaniya about a hundred miles east of Ramadi. The VHF signal was weak, and they would now be between radio stations until Amman came into range, which, according to the chart, wouldn't be until they were seventy-five miles into Jordan.

They were on their own, at least for the next forty minutes.

Peering below, Rob saw what looked like an Arab caravan of men and camels strung along an empty stretch of desert. Until now, this had just been an image in his encyclopaedia. But here was the real thing.

Albeit five miles below him.

As they continued, the meagre indications of life became fewer, but the waypoints were easier to spot as the supply route from Baghdad to Jordan left a distinct trail on the desert floor.

That made the flying unchallenging, and the previous twenty-four hours were catching up with Rob.

He'd never thought he'd feel sleepy flying a single-seat fighter jet. But here he was, with the stick held gently between his knees. He could easily nod off. Damn that irresponsible drinking session!

He kept himself awake by scanning the instruments and doubling how often he carried out his *en route* checks.

Looking at the map and then ahead, he calculated the border was now seventy miles away. He scanned the horizon, just able to pick out a settlement. Presumably Trebil.

The airflow over the canopy was a rhythmic roar, seeping into the ear cones inside his helmet.

It was as peaceful as a fighter jet could be.

Until his radio burst into life.

"I've got a problem."

13

"**F**uel regulator's packing up," Bunny said.

Rob thought quickly. It was a key component of the engine. Without it, the engine could be easily be over-fuelled, a known issue in the Venom that had been the root cause of some early losses.

Rob squeezed his transmit button. "Packing up? Is it working at all?"

"It's gone . . . Hang on. It's back!" Bunny's voice still had a sing-song nature, despite the urgency of the situation. "It's playing up, though. I'll be careful on the throttle."

"We're not in a very good place," Rob said. "Clive Nuffield warned me about the border area." He scanned left and right, but saw only empty desert either side of their track.

Even less inviting than an unpredictable border town.

He grabbed the chart and looked back across their route. They weren't quite halfway. They could get back to Ramadi quicker than pressing on to Amman.

Putting down on the outskirts of a major Iraqi town

seemed preferable to gliding to a halt next to the nomads and gypsies of Trebil.

"Shall we turn back?"

Bunny didn't respond. Rob craned his neck around to see his flight commander had backed away, off to the right.

"Bunny? Shall we head back west?" Rob's hand tightened on the stick, and he looked ahead and left to clear himself into a turn.

Again, no response.

"Bunny!"

"Calm down, old boy. I'm just going through a few checks. Might be okay. We press on."

"You're sure?"

Again, Bunny didn't reply.

Fair enough. He was busy working the issue. But Rob's instinct told him they were handling this the wrong way. If the fuel regulator was on its way out, his chances of keeping the engine alive were slim. So as long as it was working, shouldn't they be using whatever range they had to get closer to the city behind them?

He checked the town ahead again. It was Trebil, a collection of single-storey buildings stretching out either side of the north-south and east-west roads, maybe fifty miles ahead.

It was hard to make out any detail. But it didn't look big enough to have an airfield.

No signs of water for miles around it.

How did people *survive* out here?

He had a sudden vision of Bunny staggering, dehydrated, and on his last legs.

Nerves welled in Rob's stomach; his heart pounded.

They were heading into a disaster.

"Bunny, I really think we should turn back," he said again, over the radio.

"Too late," Bunny replied calmly. "Engine's gone."

Again, Rob craned his neck back, but Bunny's Venom was gone. Rob rolled his wings to the right and saw his flight commander descending, nose down to maintain flying speed.

He checked the chart again. Hobson's choice now. Trebil it was.

They had the height to make it. Just.

Rob pulled his throttle back and allowed his speed to bleed away, setting himself up wide to Bunny's left, continuing to follow him down.

They were surely out of radio range, but while he was at altitude . . .

"Pan pan, pan pan, pan pan. Habbaniya. Gauntlet One."

As expected, the radio offered nothing in return.

He scanned ahead. There was some sort of arched structure on the far side of the town. The border crossing, Rob assumed.

"What are you thinking?" he called to Bunny.

"Head for the village and see what comes up. Just need a little flat bit." Again, Bunny's nonchalant tone was disconcerting.

Rob concentrated on his own flying. He was down to one hundred twenty knots, and the Venom would stall a little below a hundred. He had to keep alert. He needed to stay close to Bunny; how would he help him once he was on the ground?

He could keep an orbit above Bunny until his fuel ran low. The Venom wasn't armed, but any would-be attackers weren't to know that.

He tried the radio again, desperate for a voice to return his call.

He tried again. "Habbaniya, this is Gauntlet One. Gauntlet Two has an engine failure. Do you read?"

Nothing.

"Too far out, old boy. But nice try." Bunny's voice came over the same frequency.

Rob looked ahead, planning his levelling point. He couldn't go too low.

Something caught his eye.

An aircraft on the ground!

An actual aircraft.

It was sat in the corner of an area on the near side of the village.

Some sort of airstrip.

"Can you see that?" Rob called.

"Spot of luck!" Bunny called back.

Rob tried to make out the lie of the land. What sort of runway option did they have?

As he got closer, it became clear the aircraft was derelict. An old Junkers, probably left over from the war.

His eyes ran along some faint markings in the soil. Some sort of rudimentary or long-abandoned landing strip.

It would have to do.

"I'll put down on this strip," Bunny said. "You carry on. I'll make my own way back once I've found some comms and alerted the boys back home."

Rob didn't like that plan at all. The odds of seeing Bunny again were remote, unless help got to him quickly.

"I'll get the Anson in the air as soon as possible." Rob said, but there was no reply. Bunny must have switched off the non-essential electrics.

Rob let his aircraft drift away to the left, giving the other

Venom plenty of space for a glide approach. He watched as the more experienced pilot turned a short final. The landing gear unfolded below the aircraft, and Rob imagined how busy Bunny would be in the cockpit.

Oddly, he saw a puff of black smoke from the engine, as if it were still running. Maybe Bunny was trying a relight, a faint hope if the engine were over-fuelled.

The Venom was high over the fence but descending quickly. Rob had to initiate a second turn to the right to keep the scene in view. He rolled out in time to see Bunny's Venom leaving a cloud of dust and sand behind him as he touched down.

It looked like a good landing.

Bunny even managed to turn the aircraft off the strip, before the last of the energy ran out and it came to a stop.

Rob continued on an orbit of the field. He watched as Bunny climbed out of the cockpit and stood by the jet.

He looked up and waved.

Rob waggled his wings.

As he rolled out to the south, he saw a cloud of dust emerge from the border crossing.

A desert yellow truck.

Police? Army?

Someone had noticed Bunny's arrival.

Rob's limited experience of the Iraqi police did not suggest it would be a welcome party.

His mind started whirring.

As he pondered, he saw a second truck, much closer to the airfield. It emerged from a scruffy group of homes on the edge of town. As he watched, two figures ran after the vehicle and jumped onto the back.

Rob descended in his jet to get a closer look and hopefully scare them off.

Down at five hundred feet, he could see the two men hanging off the back. Both had rifles over their shoulders.

"Shit."

He should fly on to Amman. He needed to get in radio range, but it was hard to leave the scene.

Rob banked his Venom into a steep turn, enjoying its agility as he fed in power. He came around again and put the truck on his nose. It was now less than a mile to the old airstrip, which at least seemed to have a security fence around it.

As he got closer, he dropped the aircraft to a hundred feet and slammed open the throttle. It was noisy in the cockpit, but would have been deafening to the men in the vehicle as he ripped the air apart a few feet above them.

He threw the jet into a climb and banked over. If the truck had stopped, it must have been for only a moment. They were on the move again.

"Goddammit!"

He continued up and turned back onto his track to Jordan, keeping the throttle at full chat.

The Venom was powerful and the climb swift.

Now and again, he looked back. He could just make out Bunny's tiny figure, next to his aircraft in a vast, abandoned airfield. And was that the truck at the gates?

As he swept over the border, he checked the progress of the truck that had left the crossing. It was maybe three miles north still.

Something else caught his eye, ten miles to the south.

Two more lorries. Dark green; also headed in a straight line to Trebil.

To Bunny?

Who was who? Rob had no idea, but a terrible feeling overcame him.

He couldn't abandon his comrade.

He carried on climbing to twenty thousand feet. Now well into Jordan, he tried again on the radio.

"Amman tower, this is Royal Air Force formation Gauntlet. Over."

After a brief wait, a scratchy voice came over the frequency. "Gauntlet. Come in, Gauntlet."

"This is Gauntlet One. We have an emergency. My colleague has carried out a forced landing near the border with Iraq. We need urgent assistance. Over."

There was an interminable pause. Rob carried out his periodic transit checks and had another look behind. He could still just make out Trebil. The border arches stood out in a desert of nothing else.

He keyed his mic. "Amman tower. Gauntlet. Did you receive? Over."

"There is someone to come. Please wait please."

Rob wasn't sure what the man meant. *Someone to come.* To come where?

What seemed like five minutes later—but might have been only forty-five seconds—an English voice came over the radio.

"Gauntlet One. Amman tower. Flight Lieutenant Jenkins speaking. Who is this?"

A wave of relief swept over Rob.

"This is Rob May of two-one-seven squadron. I'm in a Venom. My colleague is down at Trebil."

"Crashed?"

"A forced landing. He's okay, but on his own."

"Roger. We're expecting you. We have the Anson for your return. What would you like us to do?"

"You need to leave now and pick us up at Trebil."

"Pick you both up, Gauntlet One? Are you intending to land?"

"Affirmative. I need to support Flight Lieutenant Pater-Smith. He's in trouble. We have an unused cartridge in each aircraft, we might be able to get both going again."

There was no reply. Rob tentatively banked around in a shallow turn, while he waited for confirmation that the Anson was on its way.

Rob keyed the mic again. "You need to get airborne as soon as possible. There's an airstrip on the western side of the town. The Venom is there. I'll also be there, and we'll make sure the strip's cleared for you."

Another long pause.

Rob could only imagine what they were thinking. He'd directed an RAF flight to a dusty border-town airstrip where many things could go wrong.

But needs must.

Eventually, they came back on.

"Right. We've spoken to HQ. They would rather you flew on to Amman. We can pick up your friend on the way back to Habbaniya."

"Negative. He needs help now. I'm going down. We can then transit back to Amman together, maybe even with both Venoms. If we can sort Bunny's fuel pump."

It went quiet again.

After a minute of nothing, Rob steepened his bank.

"To hell with this . . ."

He rolled out with Trebil on his nose.

The radio crackled again.

"No, they're not happy. Gauntlet, you are ordered to continue to Amman. They will send out ground troops from Habbaniya for your colleague."

"You can't be serious? That will take five hours! We can't

leave him there. There's a truckload of God knows who bearing down on him now. Please check with HQ and tell them he's under attack."

Another wait. But this time, Rob was already heading back to Iraq.

"We've tried, Gauntlet, but HQ are firm, sorry."

The signal was getting weaker.

Rob locked eyes on the small border village. His head was full of images of Bunny, helplessly waving a single pistol against a lorry of local militia.

What was he getting himself into?

He didn't care. It was the right thing to do.

He took a deep breath.

"Christ's sake."

Rob keyed the mic to make one more effort to persuade them.

Just before he opened his mouth, he released the switch.

He keyed the mic again and spoke calmly.

"Amman tower, this is Gauntlet One, transmitting blind. I'm obviously out of range to receive, and I hope you can receive this from me. I'll be on the ground at Trebil, as discussed. Tango romeo echo bravo india lima, Trebil, on the Jordan-Iraq border. Rough position, lat thirty-seven decimal seven, long thirty-nine decimal zero. I should be down at an airstrip on the far western end of the settlement in one-zero minutes. We await your rescue. Please do not delay. Over and out."

He released the button and, for good measure, switched the radio frequency back to Habbaniya.

14

As Rob set himself up for an approach to the airstrip, he took another look at the situation on the ground. The first truck was at the gates to the ramshackle airfield. Bunny's Venom sat off the runway.

Trebil itself looked like a village built around the border checkpoint, a military town.

The army truck was also closing in, as were the two dark-green lorries to the south, although they were a good way off.

He banked the Venom around to set up a southerly approach.

As he rolled out, he spotted one more vehicle. A Land Rover, maybe? Someone else unknown to join the party.

With luck, at least one of these groups would be friendly.

With luck.

Scrubbing off his speed, he lined up on what passed as a runway, little more than a few ancient markings.

Remembering Habbaniya, he made sure he was at target speed early.

With flaps out and about one-third power kept on, he flew a stable approach.

At the last second, as he crossed the outer fence, he realised the runway was not as smooth as Bunny had made it look.

Too late to back out now.

Up ahead, Bunny emerged from behind his Venom, waving his arms frantically. Rob focused on his landing; a short final onto an unprepared strip in a jet-engine aircraft was not the time to take on-board hand signals.

As the Venom dropped lower, Rob felt the wheels reaching for the desert floor as a cloud of dust kicked up around him. There was a loud thud, and he braked.

The engine made a tearing noise. Panicked, he snapped the high-pressure fuel-cock to shut it down.

He kept his feet on the brakes, but the Venom seemed to have a mind of its own on the loose gravel. The nose swung right, and he countered with left rudder, before the plane oscillated and swung left. Rob quickly released his left brake to use some differential to straighten her out.

"Slow down, for God's sake!"

The jet obeyed, and the energy quickly bled off. A sprinkle of stones rattled against the fuselage as he finally came to a stop.

Then there was quiet, just a faint whine of a gyro in the background and a breeze buffeting the canopy.

It had been a violent landing for a jet-engine aircraft, and Rob suddenly felt the weight of his decision-making.

Although he had a starter cartridge ready to fire, he was now doubtful this aircraft would ever leave the ground again.

His hands shook as he carried out the after-landing

checks; he went through the list until the master power was off.

The aircraft was dead, possibly fatally wounded.

A stupid decision? At least one made for the right reasons. Bunny, alone and trapped, now had a comrade. And a signal to the would-be attackers that other RAF aircraft were coming.

Rob slid the canopy back, made his ejection seat safe, and undid his harness.

He pulled his helmet and oxygen mask off, before standing up.

Bunny stood to the side of the Venom, hands on hips.

"You fucking idiot."

15

B unny's anger took awhile to subside. He stood by as Rob closed the canopy and sealed in his flying gear, removing only his pistol.

"What were you thinking, May? That Venom can't land here, for God's sake. At the very least, you should have shut the bloody engine down before getting on the ground. You must have sucked in half the fucking desert. Bloody fool."

"I came here to help. There's a welcoming party on its way, and it doesn't look friendly."

"You were supposed to fly on to Amman. Now the base will start a search and rescue."

"They're coming here."

Bunny eyes widened. "They're doing bloody what?"

"They're coming here. I flew on long enough to get in VHF range of Amman tower, and they put the Anson pilot on."

Bunny's mouth hung open. He turned away. Rob could see his fists in tightened balls. *"Fuuuuck!"* he shouted into the wind.

Rob stumbled backwards. "What? I don't understand what's going on. It was the safest thing to do."

He watched as Bunny fought to get his temper under control. "Have you any idea what you've done?"

Rob shook his head. "No. I did this to help you. I shouldn't have bothered. I should have left you to die, at the mercy of the smugglers around here."

"You are a prize pisspot, May. A prize pisspot."

A crashing sound of metal carried on the wind. Both men turned their attentions to the main gate, which sat just beyond a couple of abandoned prefab buildings.

"I saw that truck leave the local housing area," Rob said.

Bunny walked towards the side of the runway, staring at the gate area.

Rob followed. His flight commander stood watching as the old farm vehicle drove onto the airfield, over the section of fence it had torn down.

The vehicle came to a stop, and a man got out. He wore brown robes, with a rifle over his shoulder. The two men Rob had seen jumping onto the rear of the vehicle appeared by his side. They looked around, assessing their next move. The valuable fighter jets sat just a few hundred yards away.

But they were wary.

Bunny walked into the open, his pistol drawn. Rob held his breath.

The lead man from the vehicle stood and stared. Rob joined Bunny, also drawing his gun.

For a few seconds, the two groups stared each other down.

A new noise carried across the western side of the airfield. Rob turned.

The army truck he'd seen leaving the border kicked up a cloud of dust as it raced around towards the main gate.

When he looked back, the first three men were back in their truck and pulling off, heading straight for the gate. They were more frightened of the local militia than they were of two spindly RAF officers.

"Here comes the real trouble," Bunny said, watching the army lorry. "If they get within five hundred yards, we'll loose off a couple of warning shots with the Brownings." He turned to Rob's Venom. "We need to get this thing off the runway."

"Good idea. The Anson will need the full strip," Rob said. He went back to his jet, opened the canopy, and reached in to disengage the park brake. The Venom rocked back slightly on its wheels.

He took up a spot behind the right wing. Between them, they got the aircraft moving. Built to be as light as possible and now with only half a tank of fuel, it wasn't too hard to shift.

The Venom trundled over the ground, bucking through a couple of drainage troughs like a rodeo steer. At one point, Rob heard a crack.

Once the aircraft was well clear of the old landing strip, they let it settle into another trough.

Rob was about to inspect the plane, when they heard the first gunshots.

Instinctively, he ducked, but Bunny remained upright next to him.

"Perhaps over here," he said, strolling towards a small concrete structure close to Rob's Venom.

It resembled a square well, about a yard high, but wide enough for them both to take cover behind. It probably housed a water pump.

Bunny slowly crouched down behind it.

"Be a good chap and tell me what's happening," he said.

"The army lorry has arrived. I think they must have fired at the gang."

"Where are they?"

As Rob watched, the official-looking vehicle trundled over the broken gate and parked up next to the old control tower building.

Two men with rifles emerged and stood behind the lorry. They pointed their weapons back at the gate.

Confused, Rob scanned the entrance area. In the distance, just coming into view, was the Land Rover he'd seen on the road from Ramadi.

More gunshots. Puffs of smoke from the rifles. The Land Rover ground to a halt.

The men lowered their guns.

"May? What's happening?"

"There's a Land Rover approaching, but they've fired at it."

"Is it hit?"

As Rob watched, the Land Rover began reversing, turning to its left and performing a three-point turn.

"It's still moving, but backing off."

The armed men took up position by the airfield gate. Rob scrutinised the lorry. No one else emerged.

"Don't know what's happening now. Maybe they're waiting for orders?"

Rob slumped down next to him, behind their meagre cover.

Bunny checked his watch and calmly pulled a dark cigarette case from his flying coverall. He picked out a slim cigarillo and took his time lighting it.

He took a long drag and spoke as he exhaled. "If I were to guess, I'd say the first truck was the local entrepreneurs. But now the border wallahs are here to keep the prize to themselves. Probably waiting for the nearest Mr Big to come along, divvy up the loot, and oversee our summary execution."

"Why would they do that?"

"Well, first, it's their favourite pastime. Second, those Venoms cost more than the entire town is worth. There is much to shoot someone over."

Rob looked at the aircraft. Bunny's looked more or less okay, but his own sat lower on one gear. It must have been damaged when they pushed it.

"Damn. I can't even fly mine out. What are we going to do, Bunny?"

"I thought you'd come here to rescue me." Bunny gave Rob the look a parent might give an errant teenager. He patted his pistol. "Hopefully, Mr Browning will keep them away long enough."

Rob shook his head. "The Anson will take an hour at least."

"We're not waiting for the Anson."

"Then what are we waiting for?"

A shot hit the ground and Bunny flinched, drawing his legs completely behind the water-pump housing.

Rob pulled his own legs up, making himself as small as possible.

Bunny leant out, leading with his gun. "Now the fun starts."

16

F or a while, nothing more happened.

Rob didn't dare look out from their concrete shelter, but he listened intently: the odd sound of Bunny shifting position or taking a drag mixed with the occasional voice, carrying on the wind from the gate area.

Their favourite pastime.

What kind of mentality existed out here, where men would casually execute others?

Bunny was right; Rob was an idiot. Landing here had been a bad decision. Possibly fatal. There was no doubting it now.

He hadn't chosen to rescue Bunny; he'd chosen to die with him.

The lorry engine started.

Rob sank to his knees and crept around the other side of the concrete, before quickly retreating.

"Bunny."

"Yes, old boy?"

"They're coming."

Bunny stubbed out his cigarillo. Slowly, he rolled onto

his front and shuffled so he could see around the side of the well.

Rob peered just over Bunny's head.

The lorry was driving towards them. Or, more accurately, towards the Venoms.

"Mustn't let them get too close," Bunny said, and fired his Browning at the vehicle.

The spent cartridge flew past Rob's ear, and he recoiled. "Christ alive!"

Bunny continued to peer around the concrete and fired two more shots.

Rob could hear metallic clunk sounds, as the bullets found their target.

The lorry revved.

"Seems to have done the trick," Bunny said. "They'll back off and reassess."

Rob rubbed his ringing ear and looked around the other side of the well to see the lorry had performed a U-turn and was heading back to the ramshackle buildings near the gate. He withdrew and sat down. Bunny had his head propped up on the concrete, eyes closed, with another cigarillo in his mouth.

"Can we hang on until the Anson gets here?" Rob said.

Bunny looked at his watch again. "I told you. We're not waiting for Johnny RAF to appear. We need to hold out for eight more minutes."

"I don't understand. Who's coming?"

"This is all very much above your station, May. Don't worry about it."

The wind whipped up around them, swirling grains of sand into Rob's face. He raised his arm to cover his eyes. When he put it back down, he gaped at Bunny.

The man was taking a nap.

A few minutes went by. Rob bitterly regretted his decision to come back. He'd expected to find a grateful and desperate Bunny. Instead, he found him infuriatingly calm and secretive. Had he somehow arranged a rescue using his radio?

He wanted to shake him awake and ask again about who was coming. But he already felt like a child listening into a parental conversation.

A noise rattled him from his thoughts.

Bunny's eyes remained closed; Rob crawled past him and peered out.

"It's another truck. Two of them. I think I saw these from the air. They were maybe twenty-five miles away when I was orbiting as you landed. They look new."

"What colour?" Bunny asked without moving.

"I'm sorry?"

Bunny sighed. "Are they dark green?"

Rob looked again. "Yes."

Bunny didn't respond.

The new arrivals drove over the downed security gate and onto the airfield. They rounded the buildings and accelerated directly towards Rob and Bunny's cover.

Rob looked across to the first lorry, which was on the far side of the huts and therefore blocked from the new arrivals' view.

As the green lorries cleared the buildings, they drew to a halt.

Two of the border soldiers levelled their rifles at the newcomers.

Neatly dressed soldiers wearing a light khaki jumped out of the new lorry.

The border soldiers lowered the weapons and seemed to shout back to their comrades in the old lorry.

As he watched the men, apparently caught in a moment of hesitancy, one of the border soldiers jerked and fell backwards to the ground. A spray of red leapt into the air.

The remaining soldier ran back to his truck, but was also struck by a bullet. He crashed to the ground in an ugly heap.

Rob jumped in shock and looked across to see the smartly dressed soldiers laughing.

"What's happening?" Bunny called, presumably still with his eyes shut.

"The new people are firing at the others. I think they just killed two of them." Rob's voice was croaky. A combination of the dry air and shock.

"Keep me up to date."

More men jumped out of the back of the green trucks. Rob counted at least six from the first vehicle. They walked towards the old lorry, rifles aimed. There was a sudden burst of shouting and the first arrivals emerged, one by one, from the truck, hands high in the air, standing next to their recently slain comrades.

The new soldiers had the original group lying on the ground as they disarmed them.

One man kicked a downed soldier; it was clear, even from five hundred yards, he was dead.

"They've captured them."

"Airfield secure!" Bunny said, as if making a radio call.

Rob remained crouched, with his head only just poking around the side of the concrete. The smartly dressed soldiers looked over to where the Venoms were parked. "I think we're next."

The wind whipped around the concrete structure; it sounded like a low growl.

A familiar sound.

The sound of a vintage Hawker Fury that could belong to only one man.

As the World War Two fighter swept into the circuit, Rob slowly withdrew from his crouch, stood up, and stared down at his dozing flight commander.

Contempt welled in him as everything became clear.

"For fuck's sake, Bunny."

17

B
unny opened his eyes and looked up. "Not worried about being shot at, May?"

Rob spoke slowly. "They're not going to shoot us, are they?"

Bunny looked back down, closed his eyes again, and smiled.

"Let me guess," Rob continued. "The new arrivals in the two green trucks are Prince Nuri's men?"

"They're called the Imperial Guard, rather pompously, but they are fantastically loyal. And fantastically violent, I'm led to believe."

Rob's facial features tightened. His hands clenched into fists.

"And your Venom is perfectly serviceable," he said, with his teeth barely apart. "Isn't it? You're giving it to your friend, the prince."

Bunny put one hand down and pushed himself into a crouch. He brushed off some of the desert before standing up.

"Not so much a gift as a transaction. Prince Nuri is a

wonderful combination of ambitious and incredibly rich. And he has this fanciful notion he can build alternative armed forces, loyal to his brother. He has some soldiers, some member of the Iraqi air force, but he's lacking in a few important areas."

Rob shook his head in disbelief.

"You've stolen an RAF fighter jet."

"I'm transferring a fighter from a dwindling air force whose time has well and truly passed, to a young hero in waiting." He turned to Rob. "You know they're coming for him and his brother?"

Rob threw his arms up. "So? What right does that give you to steal an extremely valuable aircraft? From the Queen, I might add."

In the distance, the prince's Hawker Fury turned onto final.

"Oh, May. Don't be so dramatic. It will be in better hands, believe me. What would Two one three Squadron do with it? Fly meaningless training sorties until one day the fuel regulator really did pack up and leave some poor sod in a hole in the desert? Better in the hands of this young man, however naive he might be. It might just save him."

Rob couldn't believe the conversation he was having.

"What's he going to do? Take on the new government with a single Venom?"

Bunny laughed. "Maybe. Look, don't take me on, old boy. Your lot have no idea what we went through. For you, all this playing sandcastles in the desert might feel like the real thing, but believe me, it's a long bloody way from getting up with a group of chaps in the morning, scared of making a friend because half of them won't be alive at teatime." He got to his feet. "You know we're just messing around out here, don't you, May? Pretending we're still an empire. And now it's over." He put a hand on Rob's shoulder. "I'm tired, Robert. I can't wear the military straitjacket any more. And I'm not going back to England for anyone."

The Fury was on the ground and rolling to a stop.

Rob put his hands over his face. "I can't believe this. What have you dragged me into?"

"Dragged you into? I sent you on to Amman to be none the wiser. This was your choice. And it's left me with a tricky situation."

The prince climbed out of his aircraft; he wore a scarf around his neck and carried a leather flying helmet.

"So, what was your great plan? How on earth were you going to get back to Habbaniya?"

"I'm not going back. You were supposed to go back. I was supposed to be missing, presumed dead." He turned and bit his lip. "But now there's two of us."

"Presumed dead? What were you planning to do?"

"May, I am still doing it, make no mistake. I will be delivered to an Assyrian household in Jordan. After that, I think I'll settle in Israel. Friendly to Europeans seeking refuge, apparently. And I suppose we'll leave you here for the Anson. If you solemnly swear to tell lies, all lies, and nothing but lies."

"And if I don't want to play your treacherous game?"

Bunny looked across to Nuri, who was talking to the group of Imperial Guards. He looked serious, handing out orders.

The militia were still pinned down on the ground. Was Nuri the real thing? Would the man he'd heard speak and even cry at last night's dinner chastise his men for murdering two locals and order them to release the others?

He appeared to ignore them.

"Look, it's easy," Bunny continued. "You tell them I'd

gone by the time you landed. They'll assume I got airborne again. They won't hang around here, believe me. You'll be back at Habbaniya before anyone realises I'm not coming home. The Venom will be written off. And so will I."

Rob shook his head. Bunny was odd and mentally unbalanced, but this plan was insanity. And it placed a huge burden on him to lie to anyone and everyone in authority.

"Nobody loses, May," Bunny started up again. "The Venom will be a footnote at the bottom of a government ledger. They'll barely notice."

18

"**D**ear chap!" Prince Nuri called as he arrived next to them. "What's this? Two Venoms?" He raised an eyebrow. "I hope you're not changing the terms, Pater-Smith."

Rob looked between Nuri and Bunny. "What?"

"Now, my dear thing," Bunny said, ignoring the question. "From my comrade's description of the exciting events around the gate, I believe my good friend and loyal servant, Asu, arrived some twenty minutes ago in an RAF Land Rover, but was rather rudely chased off by the local border wallahs."

Rob continued to look between the men as they both stared at him expectantly.

The prince cocked his head, waiting for Rob to speak.

"Mr May?"

"That was Asu? In the Land Rover?" Rob asked Bunny.

Bunny shrugged. "How else am I supposed to get to Jordan? Was he hit, May?"

A million thoughts crowded into Rob's mind. He looked

at Nuri, who raised his eyebrow, still clearly expecting his situation report.

"The vehicle was, certainly. I can't speak for the driver, but it did drive off."

"Asu resourcefully relieved the MT section of a long-range one-ten" Bunny said to the prince. "He'll be ferrying me further east in about ten minutes. If your team would be good enough to escort him back here, Your Highness?"

This would explain why Bunny had wanted to delay their departure for so long: to give Asu a chance to cross the two hundred miles from Habbaniya.

But what about the fierce row Rob had witnessed between Bunny and Asu? Had Asu somehow been forced to comply?

"Murdhi!" the prince shouted.

One of the Imperial Guardsmen turned and ran towards them, arriving with a salute. Captain stripes adorned his epaulettes.

"Sir."

"A vehicle is loitering somewhere nearby. A Land Rover with a UK mark. They need an escort onto the airfield, please."

"Yes, sir." Murdhi turned on his heels. He gathered a few of his men and jumped into a truck before heading towards the gate.

Nuri glanced at the local militia, spreadeagled on the desert floor, including two bodies. He turned back to Bunny without comment.

It dawned on Rob that he might have just seen the first shots of a civil war, a war between those elements of the Iraqi armed forces loyal to the crown and those ready to overthrow them.

"So, you bring me two jets," Nuri said. "How kind!"

He walked towards the Venoms; Bunny followed him.

The breeze picked up dust, depositing it on the shiny aircraft. Rob leant on the side of the concrete pump station and closed his eyes, trying to make sense of what was happening around him.

They certainly hadn't covered this in training.

Behind him he heard Bunny and a prince of the Iraqi royal family, sniffing around a stolen fighter jet.

He thought back to the failed dual check—probably part of Bunny's plan to keep him around. After all, he seemed to have burnt his bridges with every existing member of the squadron.

He must have licked his lips when he saw a naive tyro.

Another vehicle appeared at the gates, the largest of all. A low loader. As it trundled over the broken metal fence, Rob saw it came complete with a fork-lift truck.

The lorry came to a stop; a handful of men in grey coverall jumped out. As they approached, Nuri pointed at Bunny's Venom.

The mechanics got to work hauling pieces of specialist heavy equipment over to the aircraft. They lifted the airframe using a mobile jack, raised the undercarriage, and began work on the wings.

They knew exactly what they were doing.

Nuri caught him observing the procedure and flashed a warm smile. And yet it felt sinister. In that moment he realised he was the odd one out. Everyone else was in on the scheme. Even the reluctant Asu.

Only Rob could undo their hard, illicit work.

And he would.

Bunny may have thought Nuri's makeshift air force would make better use of the jets than an RAF squadron that faced no enemy. But that didn't make it right.

su emerged from his appropriated Land Rover, clutching his blood-soaked arm.

"Asu!" Rob ran over.

"Flying Officer May?"

"Believe me, I'm as surprised as you are to see me. What happened?"

"I was shot. I thought the men here were the prince's guards. I was wrong."

Rob urged his hand away from his arm. The wound was open at the back, with fragments of flesh hanging free. It did, at least to Rob's untrained eye, look like the bone wasn't broken.

Rob sucked in his teeth. "Is it painful?"

Asu shook his head; Rob gave him a doubtful look.

"I think we should find a tourniquet. And you'll need that wound cleaned as soon as possible." Rob headed off to the prince, who was overseeing the work on the Venoms. Bunny stood to one side, smoking.

"Excuse me, Your Highness. Do you have any medical supplies? Our friend has been shot."

Prince Nuri looked across and raised his eyebrows. "Yes, he has." He turned to his captain. "Murdhi, can you help that man, please?"

"Asu took a bullet," Rob shouted across to Bunny.

Bunny glanced over, then resumed his smoking.

Rob walked up to him. "He took a bullet for you, dammit."

"Do I detect a note of insolence in your tone, Flying Officer May?"

Rob shook his head. "Haven't you any compassion for him?"

Bunny looked over Rob's shoulder.

"He didn't take a bullet for me. He has no future at Habbaniya."

Rob studied Bunny's face. Was this an act? All this nonchalance in the face of alarming and upsetting events?

Or a sign of actual insanity.

"Asu didn't seem very cooperative this morning. I saw you two arguing."

Bunny looked surprised. He threw his cigarillo on the ground and crushed it under his black flying boot. "Well, not everyone has the spirit for a jape. He needed a little persuasion."

A noise distracted Rob, and he turned to see the interlocking wing sections pulled away from the fuselage.

"So you're not going to fly them out?" Rob asked, looking towards Prince Nuri.

"I'd prefer to preserve them in perfect flying condition. We agreed an engine-off glide onto this rough ground would be safe, but a take-off, as I'm sure you could assess, Mr May, would be far too risky."

"I'm afraid I didn't shut down my engine, so it's probably

taken a lot of damage. Perhaps you should ask for some money back?"

Nuri's expression changed.

"I see you and Mr Pater-Smith have already had a disagreement."

"My black eye? That was a mess game. But this is something different."

Nuri appeared to ponder for a second. He turned to one of his guards and waved his hand, pointing at Rob.

The soldier positioned himself behind.

The next noise Rob heard was the unmistakable sound of a gun being cocked.

20

R ob's heart thudded in his chest. Bunny slowly meandered away, leaving him on the wrong end of a Lee-Enfield rifle.

The guard held the weapon by his hips, not taking his eyes off his prisoner.

Nuri's men had already shown how casually they could kill. Rob felt certain he was next.

He'd been a fool not to realise sooner that he was in danger. His presence threatened Nuri's biggest prize in his attempt to assemble a defence force.

Surely, he would not think twice.

More noises shook Rob from his gloomy thoughts. The Venom's wings lay side-by-side on the ground. Three mechanics arranged themselves around the fuselage as another drove the fork-lift truck across the rough terrain.

They had worked incredibly fast.

After placing Bunny's plane on the low loader, along with the wings, the men had secured a tarpaulin over it, then used a second cover to throw over the remains of Rob's aircraft.

Rob stared at his aircraft's final resting place. A valuable fighter jet would now, in Clive Nuffield's words, be little more than a chicken coop.

Nuri organised his guardsmen, issuing instructions to four of the twelve who'd arrived in the two lorries.

But one guardsman remained behind with Rob, rifle in hand.

Bunny glanced at the sky and shouted over to Rob. "May, what time was your last contact with the Anson captain?"

Rob checked his watch. "About four."

"Hmm. They'll be hurrying along to beat the sunset." He nodded towards Nuri. "Now would be a good time to get on the road."

Nuri walked over to Bunny with a broad smile on his face. "Then I must say goodbye to my dear friend. You're certain I cannot take you with me to Baghdad? It would be useful to have your experience alongside us. And you know I pay well."

Bunny shook his head. "Thank you, Nuri. Asu will take me across the border. The sooner I'm out of Iraq, the better. I only hope the same is not true for you, my friend."

Nuri laughed. "Don't you worry about me. At the very least, I have a fast taxi now."

Nuri put his hands on Bunny's shoulders. "You have been a good friend. And a loyal subject. Goodbye, Flight Lieutenant Pater-Smith."

Nuri made his way towards the lorry carrying his precious cargo. He wanted to keep a close eye on his bounty.

Bunny headed to his waiting ride with Asu. He turned to Rob.

"You'll be fine, May. Anson will arrive within the half hour. Safe travels. Remember. *Missing, presumed dead.*" Bunny waved a hand in the air as he walked away.

The low loader started up and shifted from its position, keeping a slow, measured rate across the airfield, until it disappeared behind the old tower.

Rob dared to feel relieved. No summary execution.

He looked to the skies. How long before the Anson arrived? Would the local army men be left alone with him? Not a happy prospect; he would be blamed for the deaths of their comrades.

He watched the guards as they climbed back on board their two lorries, then checked the time.

Just as he looked at his watch, a sharp prod in his back knocked him forward. He stumbled, but before he could look behind him, he felt another.

"Move!" a gruff voice said.

He spun around to see the guard level his rifle at him.

"Now!" the man shouted.

He started walking as ordered.

"What's going on?"

One lorry was already on the move, but the last one remained. Soldiers climbed onto the rear gate and up into its interior.

The guard pushed Rob towards it.

"Bunny!" Rob shouted.

Bunny was about to get into Asu's Land Rover. He glanced over and shouted at the guards.

"I say. What's going on?"

The guard continually prodded Rob to keep him moving.

"Does the prince know about this?" Bunny shouted.

This was greeted by laughter from the back of the lorry.

"He can come with us," Bunny shouted as he marched towards them. But a guard quickly jumped out of the lorry and blocked his path.

"Move out of the way!" Bunny said, in a firm voice, which had no effect at all.

The guard pushing Rob along ordered him into the lorry and then turned to Bunny. "I have my orders. Stay back, sir."

"No, no. I'll take care of it," Bunny shouted over the noise of the lorry starting.

The guard shoved Rob onto one of the hard metal bench seats that ran down either side of the cargo area. Soldiers were pressed against him on both sides.

"Robert!" Bunny's cry from outside. "Get him out of there!"

The final guard climbed into the lorry, casually cocked his rifle, took aim at Bunny and fired.

21

A tarpaulin cover dropped into place as the lorry pulled out of the airfield, plunging the interior into darkness.

Rob just had time to see Asu running towards Bunny, but his body was lifeless. Asu looked up, his face torn with distress.

Of all the tasks Asu had taken on, it was clear that protecting Bunny from himself was his priority. With his last act, Bunny didn't even have the grace to spare Asu from failure.

In the darkness, Rob shed quiet tears for a man he barely knew. And a man who would probably cost Rob his own life before the day was out. He had to assume they were taking him somewhere his body would never be found.

Missing, presumed dead.

THE LORRY HAD BEEN MOVING for about an hour, no doubt on the road back to Baghdad, although Rob, sitting in the darkness, couldn't be certain.

He sat motionless, unable to do anything but accept his fate.

The men around him ate from a large steel pot set up among them. It stank of stale meat. Suddenly the man to Rob's right ordered him to switch places, pushing him to the rear of the truck, while he greedily spooned cold, dark stew into his mouth.

Looking down, Rob saw a gap in the tarpaulin.

For the first time in a while, his mood lifted, very slightly.

He couldn't be passive until the bullet was inevitably fired at his head.

If there was a chance, however slim, what did he have to lose?

The opening was at the base of the rear canvas where the material wasn't quite large enough to meet the bottom of the lorry. Through the gap, Rob could just see the road, bathed in the last rays of sunset. So they were travelling east, as he suspected. Ramadi was the first town they would reach.

He glanced down again.

Was the canvas loose enough for him to escape once it was dark?

He didn't give himself great odds, but running into the desert was the best option he could think of.

He gently pushed at the material; it wasn't taut, but it snagged on the ropes instantly. The gap was far too small for him.

He considered his embryonic plan. Even if he made it away, he would stand out a mile in the flat, desolate landscape.

Maybe as they got closer to the city, with houses either

side of the road, he would stand a better chance of disappearing.

Rob shuffled his legs, but couldn't get comfortable. He could see why he'd been ordered to swap places; there was cargo beneath his feet.

The interior of the truck was noisy, and the men filled up with food and chatted loudly.

Exhaust fumes curled up from the back of the lorry, making him nauseous.

His legs cramped. Again, he shuffled his feet. But they kept knocking against the cargo container. He looked down; it was a pair of jerry cans, bound together.

A prerequisite of desert driving.

He tested their weight with his feet. They were both full, a precious commodity that saved lives.

Without appearing to alter his behaviour, he took more care to note his surroundings.

The noise level ramped up. Apparently, nothing raised spirits like a cold goat stew.

A new plan formed.

Without looking down, he dropped his right hand and felt the top of the cans. The catches, common to all jerry cans, were familiar enough. He stole a glance.

If he could manoeuvre the bundle so the ends overhung the gap in the tarpaulin, he could crack open the lids and empty them over the side.

He wasn't sure exactly what would happen when they ran out of fuel, but it might just offer an opportunity.

Rob gave the cans a firm push with his feet and one hand, which he lowered into the shadows.

As he did so, the truck hit a pothole, and the entire lorry seemed to jump.

The can stabbed up into his hand, and Rob just about suppressed a yelp of pain.

One guardsman turned and stared at him, but he adopted a normal expression.

The man went back to his shouted conversation with the soldier next to him.

A moment later, they hit a second rut. As the lorry bounced up, Rob used the momentum to shove the cans towards the back.

He stole another glance. They were right on the edge, hanging over enough, but resting on their sides, with the lids at ninety degrees.

He needed to spin them around.

The road grew rougher. Each jolt enabled him to shift them further.

The next pothole was substantial; everyone lurched, and Rob had to steady himself on his neighbour. As he did so, he heard a faint thud on the road behind.

No one else seemed to notice.

When the lorry settled and he looked back down, the jerry cans were gone.

Rob froze, not daring to look up.

Slowly, he leant back and, as casually as he could, looked around him.

No one was paying him any attention, not even the guard opposite, who had spent the first part of the journey glowering at him.

He let out a long breath. Throwing the cans overboard wasn't the plan, but it served the same purpose.

Daylight was almost gone, but his luminescent RAF watch told him they'd been on the road for an hour and a half.

Rob sat back, closed his eyes.

He pictured a dank dungeon in a royal palace, and the sudden darkness of a bullet in the back of the head.

He opened his eyes. He couldn't simply wait for whatever they had planned for him.

The fuel ruse might lead to something, but what if it didn't? What if the cans had been spares, and they had enough in the tanks to get to Baghdad?

He needed to go back to the tarpaulin gap. Could he make it bigger and slip out as they slept around him?

He'd hit the ground hard, but he'd take his chances with that.

Around him, men drifted off, replete after dinner. The guard opposite him, annoyingly, remained awake and occasionally looked his way.

Rob closed his eyes and lolled his head back against the taut canvas, holding the position. He feigned sleep, but silently counted the seconds.

He stayed like this for a full five minutes.

The sound of the truck settled into a steady rhythm, and it was all he could do not drift off.

When he felt enough time had passed, Rob slowly opened his eyes.

His ruse had worked; the guard opposite him was asleep.

He carefully looked around. It was too dark to be sure, but it appeared as if the other ten men were also sleeping.

He reached down and pulled at the tarpaulin again.

It moved up a few inches. He used his foot to try to unstick a rubber T-bung. It worked, but widened the gap by only an inch. Not enough.

He looked over his shoulder and studied the other ties

that held it in place. More T-shaped rubber bungs, pulled into a latch.

If he could silently release two more, that should be enough.

One more glance around the truck. All was quiet. He moved his hand to the next T-bung and pulled it gently until it released. The canvas flapped in the wind, introducing a subtly different noise to the lorry interior.

He snapped his hand back and looked around. The guards slept.

Looking down again, he was now confident he'd be able to slip out.

As he contemplated the escape, he realised something else.

The lorry had sped up.

They now seemed to be on tarmac.

That made it challenging. If he fell out of the back, he could break his neck. Even a broken leg would make the rest of his escape plan impossible.

But what choice did he have? Wouldn't a broken leg be better than a bullet in the head?

This is a chance. Take it.

As quietly as he could, he shifted his backside to the edge of the bench seat. He moved both legs around and rested them on the very edge.

He would have to slip out feet first and try to roll with the motion when he hit the ground. If he got the exit right, he wouldn't disturb anyone inside, giving him precious minutes to get away from the road. If he could still walk.

Rob stared at the darkness visible through the flapping canvas. He was now perched on the very edge of the seat, dangling both feet over. It was just a matter of shifting himself off the seat and falling out.

The lorry slowed and moved across the road. Avoiding something.

This was his chance.

He placed both hands next to his side and pushed.

22

A heavy hand landed on Rob's shoulder, dragging him back into the middle of the lorry.

He crashed into the pot of stew, which partially upended onto him.

Sticky, smelly lumps of goat splashed over his face and flying coveralls.

A kick landed on his back, and he recoiled. He lifted his hands to his face to wipe off the food as more blows came in. One caught him square in the stomach and he hunched together, winded, desperately trying to catch his breath while also curling into a ball for protection.

Laughter on all sides.

The idiot Englishman and his daring escape plan . . .

Rob pulled himself into a tight ball and cried.

Was this it? Instead of escaping, he'd accelerated his demise.

An image of his mother flashed into his mind. Wearing her Sunday best, walking back from church in Fleet.

"I want to go home!" he cried to himself.

The kicks subsided. A pair of hands yanked him up and

sat him back on the bench. This time, he was in the middle of the row.

He used his sleeve to clean off as much of the stew as he could. It was cold and had already started to congeal and mat in his hair.

Rob stared into the dark void, avoiding eye contact.

He closed his eyes and dreamed of a hot shower in the Habbaniya mess. Tears mixed with the dirt, forming layers of crust below his eyes.

More time passed. A wave of mental exhaustion overcame him, but he had to stay awake. Stay alert.

He wasn't dead yet.

A change in the ambient noise stirred him from his meditative state.

He sat upright and blinked a few times.

They came to a stop and switched off the engine.

A noise came from behind, as someone yanked up the canvas. There were lights outside—a small settlement—but it was now the dead of night.

Several men jumped out, leaving him with two guards.

The men pulled tools and spare canvas from under the seats at the rear. Their voices, in Arabic, becoming increasingly agitated.

Rob kept his head bowed, but allowed himself the faintest smile.

They grabbed him and pulled him off the bench seat, then pushed him out of the truck as the search for the jerry cans expanded into the cargo area.

Rob stood to one side, taking in his surroundings. The men were distracted, lambasting one another. He didn't know any Arabic, but they seemed to blame one another for the loss.

One man slapped another, hard across the face. Others pulled him back.

Rob took a step away from the scene, into the shadows in the middle of the wide road. It was forty yards to a line of small dwellings on the far side. Somewhere for him to melt into.

He looked up and down the road, only faintly lit by a half moon. A mile or so back the way they came, a pair of headlights flickered.

That might be the distraction he needed. The men were bound to flag the vehicle down and most likely steal any fuel at gunpoint.

Once they'd filled up, it would be back into the truck.

He'd never have an opportunity like this again.

He studied the round-topped homes beyond the road. They went back maybe two hundred yards to a collection of fifty-odd buildings, some just small huts.

Beyond the back of the houses was a metal structure that looked like a pump over a well. It would explain a settlement in the middle of the desert.

He tried to do some calculations. It was about two hundred fifty miles from Baghdad to Trebil. He checked his watch and estimated they'd been driving for two and a half hours. The lorry didn't move fast.

There was still three more hours left to the capital.

Inside the lorry, the guards opened up the bench seats and emptied them. Men crawled around with torches, searching every corner for the missing fuel.

Rob tried to work out who was who in the group. One man wore sergeant stripes. He'd been riding up front and was clearly in charge. The prince, of course, was in the larger lorry, close to his new acquisition. They were somewhere ahead.

The guards' focus was on the missing cans. Was anyone watching him?

Rob looked behind. A soldier stood a few feet away, directly between him and his only escape route. *When did he turn up?*

He looked back down the road; the approaching vehicle was nearly upon them.

The lights were close together, either side of the front grille, a distinctive arrangement.

A Land Rover.

23

T he new man behind Rob moved to the middle of the road and raised a hand to stop the approaching vehicle.

Rob squinted. There wasn't enough ambient light to make out the driver, but he could just see a light-coloured uniform.

As the Land Rover got closer, the driver gunned the engine. The guard realised too late what was about to happen. He tried to run, but the car hit him.

Rob stumbled backwards against the lorry as the collision hurled the man up into the air. He fell into a crooked, bent heap on the ground behind the vehicle.

The Land Rover ground to a halt in the shadow cast by the lorry, twenty yards ahead of Rob.

The driver emerged, from the far side of the vehicle, one arm in a sling. He waved a pistol.

"Please. Quickly!" Asu shouted.

Rob ran at the Land Rover.

Shouts went up behind him. Most of the guards watched

from the other side of the lorry, shouting in anger and confusion.

The first shots whistled past Rob as he reached the Land Rover.

Asu ushered him in and shoved him across to the driving seat. He fired two shots towards the guards, then fell into the car, yelping as he landed on his arm.

"Drive, please! Flying Officer May!"

Sparks flew off the Land Rover door as Rob reached across to pull it shut.

He shoved the vehicle into first gear and hit the accelerator, spinning the wheels on the old tarmac, holding a line that put the bulk of the lorry between them and the guards.

They cleared the lorry, but more shots came in, clattering into the Land Rover's bodywork.

They pulled away, and the bullets stopped.

Rob looked into the vibrating wing mirror, dazzled as the lights of the lorry came on.

Asu was now upright and scrutinising the wing mirror on his side.

"They'll follow us, but be out of fuel soon," Rob said. "We just need to keep going. There's no way they'll get to Ramadi."

Asu slumped back in his seat. "As fast as you can, Mr Robert. Please. They are fierce men and will kill us if they catch us."

Rob focused on keeping the Land Rover in a straight line. He stole a glance at Asu; he didn't look well.

"You drove all this way with one arm?"

Asu didn't reply.

"We have to get you treated."

"Yes, sir. We will go to a place I know in Ramadi. I have an uncle. He will save Flight Lieutenant Pater-Smith."

It took a moment for Rob to process what Asu had said. Slowly, he turned his head and looked into the back of the vehicle, to see Bunny lying on his side, his arms clutched to his chest.

"He's still alive?"

"Yes, sir. But the bullet has caused very much damage. He must have help soon."

Rob faced ahead. He couldn't go any faster, but he could make sure he kept the Land Rover upright. He tried to remember Ramadi from his navigation planning. It was just east of Baghdad. He estimated another hour at least.

"We have enough fuel?"

Again, Asu didn't reply. He was too weak.

Rob looked down at the fuel gauge. Around a third remaining. Should be enough.

The miles passed, and the roadside grew busier with settlements.

"I can't believe I got away from them, Asu. You got me away."

"I didn't know what would happen when I got to you," Asu rasped. "I was lucky you had stopped. A miracle."

Of all the things Rob had done that day, offloading the fuel may have been his finest achievement.

Eventually, they passed a white sign in Arabic.

"Ramadi," Asu said.

Rob looked into the back again. He couldn't tell whether Bunny was still breathing.

"Where are we going?" Rob asked.

"Keep on until you cross the river, then go to the left. Only two miles from there."

Despite the late hour, Ramadi was still busy. They crossed a narrow bridge over the Euphrates and slowed behind a handcart pushed by two men. On the far side, Rob turned left and headed up a straight road that passed a patch of scrub-land.

Beyond that, Asu directed him off the main track, along a road that hugged a small lake.

It was a quiet, dark part of the city.

The road was potholed and narrow, with a drainage ditch between them and the lake on one side, and a row of steep-walled compounds on the other.

Rob crept along, not wanting to throw his injured passengers around more than needed.

"Here!" Asu shouted and pointed at one of the similar-looking walls. Rob turned the Land Rover in, and the head-lights swept over a battered wooden door below a painted red cross.

24

The door was battered and half open, with one side hanging off its hinges.

Beyond it, Rob could make out a large house with a set of steps to a front door.

He switched off the engine and leapt out, hurrying to the back of the Land Rover.

Asu hobbled through to the compound.

As Rob opened the Land Rover's rear door, Bunny flinched. He climbed in and crouched over him, resting a hand gently on his shoulder. Bunny's flying coverall was cold and wet.

Even in the barely lit interior, he could tell his hand was covered in blood.

"Bunny," he whispered.

In the stillness, he heard the faintest of noises, a regular, shallow wheeze and a soft bubbling.

Bunny had dark liquid around his mouth.

Arabic voices outside, coming closer.

As Rob backed out of the vehicle, Asu presented an older man in a long grey robe.

"This is Garsa."

He carried a leather case, typical for a doctor. As Rob waited, the older man fished out a pair of round spectacles, wrapping the bendy metal behind his ears.

"You're a qualified doctor?" Rob asked.

The man gave a polite laugh.

"Yes. University Hospital, Vienna," Garsa answered in perfect English. "Can I see your friend, please?"

The doctor climbed in and crouched over Bunny, studying him, before pulling a stethoscope from his bag. He placed the metal disc on Bunny's back and then his chest. He carefully undid the top of Bunny's coverall, but left him on his side. Rob watched as the doctor's hands moved over Bunny's chest. He had no light and was working by touch.

Garsa winced as he found the wound.

After a couple of minutes, the doctor climbed out.

"Asu, I will be better treating you."

"No, sir, please. Mr Pater-Smith first. You must save him."

Asu was trying to sound healthier than he was.

Garsa looked at Asu's arm, then nodded. "Very well. Please wake Adorina and my daughter. Tell them to bring the stretcher."

Asu disappeared back into the compound. In the silence, Rob heard more gurgling from within the vehicle.

"Will he live?" he asked the doctor.

Garsa spoke softly. "He will not see another sunrise."

Rob bowed his head.

They stood in silence.

After an eternity, two figures emerged from the doorway, carrying a wooden stretcher between them. A woman with a white shawl and a girl who looked barely twelve years old.

"We need to be gentle," Garsa said. "Helga, please enter

the vehicle and go to the patient's head. Lift him on. Please be very careful."

The child entered the Land Rover, easing herself around Bunny.

Garsa and Adorina expertly fed in the stretcher, partially tilted, to make it easier to roll Bunny onto it.

For the first time, Rob heard a more human noise from his flight commander, a moan and exhalation of air. But it was accompanied by a sudden cough and a horrendous splutter of blood.

"He's choking on his blood," Rob said.

"I will make him comfortable as soon as we're inside," Garsa replied.

He said something in Arabic, and Rob took a step back as the three family members eased Bunny on his front, with head tilted down and to the side.

The doctor turned to Rob. "We must keep his mouth turned downwards."

Rob stepped forward and took one corner of the stretcher. Helga, only a slight girl, somehow lifted the stretcher enough to inch it out.

Soon, Adorina joined her daughter at the head end, and the four of them lifted Bunny out of the Land Rover.

After stabilising for a second, and making sure Helga had both feet on the ground, they moved towards the wooden doorway.

It was a dilapidated place, with basket chairs and ancient medical paraphernalia strewn about the yard.

The stretcher party continued up the steps into the house, with Garsa deftly opening the double doors with his feet.

It was even darker inside. Rob navigated the threshold step, and they took Bunny into a large room on the left. In

the centre was a table, presumably used for medical procedures. It was wooden and not out of place in a dining room.
Maybe it doubled up.

The place smelled of iodine and alcohol.

But it was well ordered. Shelves with bottles in neat
rows. Stacks of clean dressings laid out, presumably ready
for the day ahead.

They shifted either side of the table and gently placed
the stretcher down.

Garsa moved away and switched on a light. The three of
them recoiled at the sight.

So much blood.

The top half of Bunny's clothing was soaked. His face
was grey and his eyes were open, staring at nothing.

Blood had congealed around his mouth and ears.

Garsa got to work, with Adorina handing him swabs and
alcohol bottles.

The doctor rolled Bunny gently onto his back, and his
head lolled to one side.

He cleaned out his mouth and ensured his airway was
clear.

Rob moved to the far side of the table and tried to make
eye contact with his commander.

"Bunny! Can you hear me?"

Slowly, Bunny's eyes seemed to focus. Rob smiled
at him.

On the other side of the table, Garsa began winding
bandages tightly around Bunny's right leg.

"What's that?" Rob asked.

"He's lost much blood. It's his only chance. We must
force the blood to his head. His body is closing down."

Bunny's weak, raspy voice made a sound.

"Asu . . ."

"It's Rob May," Rob said, kneeling down to be at eye level.

Bunny's mouth moved to form the faintest of smiles. Or possibly a wince. Rob couldn't be sure.

"Robert."

"The doctor is helping you."

But Bunny's eyes told Rob everything he needed to know. Bunny knew he was dying. A few moments left.

"I'm sorry Bunny."

He watched as Bunny tried to speak, but couldn't seem to find the energy.

Garsa leaned over and checked Bunny's eyes, before moving back to wind bandages on to his other leg.

"I think we buy him time only." He said as he pulled the bandage taut.

Rob watched, transfixed. Bunny's eyes widened. He moved his hand to Rob's, and clasped it.

Suddenly Bunny tried to sit up.

"No, no." Garsa reached over, pushing him back down. "Easy, my friend. Easy."

Rob squeezed Bunny's hand.

Bunny's head settled back on the table; he turned and stared at Rob.

"Tell them I'm sorry."

"Who, Bunny?"

"I was not . . ."

Rob waited for the sentence to finish. "Not what, Bunny?"

Bunny's face relaxed. He smiled. "I wasn't strong enough for them."

Rob exchanged a glance with Garsa.

When he looked back at Bunny, the life had left his eyes.

The brief moment of blood to his brain had induced a final moment of half consciousness.

Garsa appeared over Bunny, pressing his stethoscope against his chest in three different places, before moving around to Rob's side. Rob stepped out of the way while the doctor pushed his cheek within millimetres of Bunny's mouth.

Slowly, he stood up.

"I'm sorry."

25

A dorina pulled a dark blanket out of a chest from the far corner of the room.

She covered the body, but left Bunny's head and shoulders exposed.

"Would you like some time to say your goodbyes?" she said to Rob.

He stood staring at his flight commander, a man he'd known for three days. Tears ran from his exhausted eyes.

He looked up at Garsa. "Please, Doctor. See Asu. He needs you."

Garsa nodded and left the room, along with Adorina and Helga.

What a place for a child.

Rob didn't move. He listened as Garsa examined Asu, on the other side of the door.

Rob reached out a hand and gently stroked Bunny's cheek. He positioned his head, so he was facing up.

His open eyes were disconcerting, and Rob tried to close them. But they opened again immediately.

Rob stood in silence for a minute more.

Unsure of what else to do, he quietly recited the Lord's Prayer.

Finally, he bent down and put a hand on Bunny's forehead and stroked his hair back.

"What happened to you?" he whispered.

26

I n the small kitchen at the back of the ground floor, Adorina offered Rob some food. But he had no appetite and accepted only a cup of tea. There was no milk or sugar, so the doctor's wife stirred in a spoon of honey.

She pulled out a seat at a rickety table, and Rob sat down, cupping the warm drink. His hands were shaking from the cold, the shock, or both.

He took a sip of the sweet, soft drink, which tasted like nothing he'd tasted before, and closed his eyes, letting it soothe his dry throat.

When he opened them again, Adorina was sitting opposite. He looked around at the room. Freshly washed bandages hung from hooks near an outside door. Other medical supplies, including bottles of medicines Rob couldn't identify, sat in neat piles on a small side table. Despite the poverty of the surgery, Adorina kept an orderly house.

"Is there a hospital nearby?" Rob asked.

"There's a small one here in Ramadi and a larger one in Baghdad. But not for the likes of us."

Rob nodded. "You are Assyrians?"

"We have this place only because my husband is a valued person."

Rob could only imagine what a Western-educated doctor was worth in Ramadi.

"Tell me, does he treat only Assyrians?"

She shook her head. "Not at all. He would be arrested if he turned away someone just because they were Iraqi."

"But you said the hospitals won't treat you."

Adorina smiled and sipped her drink. "Welcome to the new Iraq."

They drank their tea in silence. Adorina didn't ask about Bunny, and Rob didn't explain.

She finished her drink and stood up.

"I will wrap him," she announced and disappeared next door.

Fifteen minutes later, Garsa called Rob to help lift the stretcher.

The four of them again took a handle each. Bunny's body was tightly wrapped with an outer layer of dark blankets-to hide the blood, Adorina told him.

With the body safely in the Land Rover, Rob stood next to the open rear door and looked up to see streaks of orange low on the horizon to the southeast.

It was still chilly, and he hugged himself.

It was hard not to keep looking at the bundle of sheets and blankets containing the remains of his flight commander.

Garsa gave Asu's sling one final inspection.

"It will heal, but it needs time without strenuous activity.

I think that is against your nature, though, Asu!" The doctor laughed.

Asu smiled. "There is always much to do, but I promise to ask others to do the lifting."

Garsa turned to Rob.

"And I think maybe you need some rest, too."

Rob took a deep gulp of morning air.

"I suspect I'll be flying a Venom to Cyprus later today."

Garsa raised an eyebrow. "You're leaving us?"

Rob nodded. "Did Asu not tell you?" He looked across to Bunny's former batman, who shook his head.

"I never discuss Royal Air Force business, sir."

"I see. Well, you may as well know, doctor. It won't be a secret after today. The whole Royal Air Force detachment is departing, I'm afraid."

"Asked to leave by our government?"

Rob shrugged. "I believe so. I'm afraid I know little about what went on. The treaty is running out, and they've refused to renew it. Something like that." He looked back to the still-open rear door on the Land Rover. "Listen, you're sure I don't have to report this to the local police?"

"I believe under the treaty you refer to, all such matters involving RAF personnel must be dealt with by your people." He paused, and Rob sensed he was choosing his words carefully. "What will you tell them?"

"The truth. What choice do I have? I'll have to explain two missing Venoms and one dead RAF officer."

Garsa nodded slowly. "You must do what you believe is right, of course."

Rob studied the doctor in the yellowing sunrise. Half shaven, with worry lines etched into his forehead. He was maybe forty years old, but he could be ten years younger and just aged by his circumstances.

"You think I should lie?" Rob asked. He glanced to his left to see Asu, loitering by the passenger door to the Land Rover, taking everything in.

"It will probably do for the Iraqi royal family," Garsa said. "A scandal such as this. They are already in a precarious position. And of course it will leave Flight Lieutenant Pater-Smith's reputation in tatters. His widow might not receive a pension." He smiled. "But that is not your concern, of course. What will be will be."

"I believe it's always better to be truthful," Rob said. "I'm not a very good liar. He died alone. No wife, no children."

"Of course." Garsa nodded.

"We should go," Asu said, and he climbed into the vehicle.

Rob nodded and held out a hand. "Thank you, Doctor."

"My pleasure, Robert."

As Rob climbed behind the wheel, he took in the street; it looked a lot worse in the sunlight. Rubbish littered the sides of the road, along with discarded glass and rotting food. It was the last place you'd want to come for medical treatment.

And the last place you'd want to die.

Adorina appeared by the side of the Land Rover. Rob pulled down the window.

"I have cooked you some eggs. For the journey."

"That is very kind," Rob said, taking a small package wrapped in cloth.

"Do I owe you anything?" Rob asked of Adorina and Garsa. "For the treatment?"

They laughed. "Do you have any anaesthetic? Or maybe a clean operating table?" Garsa replied.

"Or maybe a junior doctor or a qualified nurse?" Adorina added.

Rob smiled. "I'm afraid I'm all out."

"Ah, well. Maybe next time." Adorina held up a hand to say goodbye.

Rob shifted the Land Rover into first and pulled away, turning around to retrace their path back to the main route through the city.

As they got to the end of the junction, something shifted in the back. Rob craned his neck around.

A loose satchel had hit the rear door with a solid thud.

27

The route out of Ramadi took them through a smarter part of town. Rob had learned that Iraqi cities were divided by race: Iraqis in the nicest areas, with the best jobs and businesses; Assyrians and assorted others kept at arm's length and exploited for their services, like Garsa, with his rare medical qualification.

Despite his skill and dedication, he would never live in one of the larger houses.

Soon, the homes gave way to a more open area of country. Still, the land between Ramadi and Baghdad was more populous than before, with regular settlements, wells, and basic services. Nothing like the long stretches of emptiness that filled the east of the country.

Bunny had certainly chosen a desolate place for his clandestine meeting.

Planned in a hurry, it had almost worked.

Rob thought back to his decision to land. If he'd continued to Amman, the deal would have gone through without the complication of a witness.

And Bunny would still be alive, making his way to Israel.

He looked at Asu.

"It's the money, isn't it? In the satchel?"

Asu nodded.

They headed towards the rising sun. The roads were at their best around the capital.

"Thank you, Asu," Rob said after a moment of silence.

"For what, please, sir?"

Rob laughed at the question. "For saving my life! And for doing your best to save Bunny."

He shifted down a gear to navigate between two cattle-drawn carts.

"I serve the officers of the Royal Air Force," Asu said.

He always spoke in such clear terms. But life would be far from simple for him.

Rob pondered Garsa's hint that he should cover up what happened. He had been determined to cleanse himself of this episode by telling all. He needed to walk away with a clear conscience and with no complications.

But the doctor's gently spoken words lingered.

He knew little about the politics of Iraq, but, as Garsa had suggested, it was likely there would be consequences of this episode coming to light.

He glanced at Asu; he was still awake.

"What do you think I should tell them?"

The Assyrian turned his head and looked into the back, where Bunny's tightly wrapped body lay motionless in the centre of the vehicle.

He turned back to Rob. "It was my duty to protect Flight Lieutenant Pater-Smith in life and now in death. He is a man who needs to be helped. He does not always help himself."

"So, you think I should cover up what he did? And lie?"

"What good would come of the truth, sir, if you do not mind me asking?"

"Some might argue that regardless of consequence, the truth is always the right path," Rob said.

I sound like a vicar giving a sermon.

Asu gave a rare smile. "I'm afraid life has shown me otherwise. If you report this truth, it will begin an investigation that could bring down the royal family. You would be detained in Iraq. Not allowed to leave with your squadron. And I would be arrested as a collaborator. I cannot think of a good that comes of it. At this moment, Prince Nuri is ordering his guards to track me down and kill me. It is not a concern of yours, of course, sir, but I would rather not help them know who I am."

Rob didn't reply.

At a crossroads, Rob took the sign for Fallujah and they passed the first sign that an RAF station lay ahead, as a British transport aircraft—a Beverley—lumbered low overhead. It climbed into the morning sky, no doubt laden with what was left of three squadrons. They both watched it until it disappeared over the top of the Land Rover.

Rob pulled the vehicle to a stop and looked at Asu. "So? If I don't tell the truth, what the hell do I tell them?"

Once again, Asu looked into the back. "We can have a story, sir. But you need to do something first, before we get to Habbaniya."

"What is that, Asu?"

"You must hide the gold."

28

As they turned off the main drag and onto the long track that led to the RAF Habbaniya security gate, a column of trucks passed, going the other way.

Asu donned his tunic. He removed his sling and slotted his injured arm through the sleeve. It must have hurt like hell, but he barely winced.

Without examining him, no one would see the wound.

The gate area was alive with Levies soldiers busy with clipboards and whistles.

Rob pulled up to the entrance barrier, which remained down, blocking their path.

He drummed his hand on the steering wheel.

"They will not stop us here," Asu said.

A guard appeared at Rob's window. He gave a smart salute and leant down. His expression changed when he saw Asu.

"Good morning, sir. Good morning, Asu, my friend!"

"Good morning," Asu said. "I have been escorting Flying Officer May on important business."

"You are injured?" the guard asked, raising his eyebrows.

"It is nothing," Asu replied and waved his good hand. "I still have this one."

"Ha! Asu with one arm is worth ten men with two." The guard moved off and raised the barrier without further interrogation.

They drove on to the small medical centre.

Inside the single-storey building, Rob found two men in white coats with three nurses, all of them packing supplies into two large crates. They looked stressed at being up so early and were clearly in a hurry.

Rob coughed.

A doctor struggling with a pile of medical books looked up and immediately grimaced.

"I hope somebody's dead, young man. We're rather busy trying to make our plane."

Rob was suddenly lost for words.

The doctor slowly put down the books. "Someone is dead?"

ROB STOOD to the side as two orderlies wheeled a gurney to the back of the Land Rover, supervised by the doctor.

They eased Bunny's body out and wheeled the gurney into the medical centre.

A second doctor emerged from the practice and addressed Rob.

"I've spoken to the RAF police sergeant. You're to go straight there. Do you know where the police station is?"

"I do, sir," Asu said, from his position behind Rob.

"Very good. Don't dilly-dally. They have informed your squadron already. There's a search party out looking for you."

29

They didn't drive straight to the police station. Instead, Rob turned right and headed up to the officers' mess.

Asu walked into the building, with the satchel over his good shoulder. Rob had been surprised by the weight when he'd first tried to lift it out of the vehicle.

As he waited, he saw two figures in flying coveralls in the wing mirror, heading for the mess. Rob started the vehicle and drove up to the large car park on the far side. He waited a minute before driving back.

The men—Nuffield was one—had disappeared.

Asu waited on the kerb, urgently looking left and right.

JUST LIKE THE MEDICAL CENTRE, the inside of the police station was bare.

As Rob waited in the reception area, a group of Levies NCOs shuffled past, carrying crates.

Every building on Habbaniya was slowly emptying.

A police sergeant in desert fatigues with a red band around his arm led Rob into a small interview room.

He opened a notepad that already had a page of handwriting.

"So, Flight Lieutenant Jenkins has given us his side of what happened," he said in a London accent that contained few *T* sounds.

Rob was momentarily confused. Who the hell was Jenkins?

The policeman scanned his notes, using his pen to find the relevant sections. He glanced up and saw the look on Rob's face. "Jenkins was at Amman, and you two spoke on the radio, apparently," he paused. "He rather thinks you disobeyed an order."

Rob fixed the man with what he hoped was a confident look. "I had no choice. Flight Lieutenant Pater-Smith was coming under attack. I couldn't leave him. Besides, the signal was patchy, and I wasn't clear what the order was."

The man looked doubtful. "Well, the evidence does support the your belief that Flight Lieutenant Pater-Smith was in danger, I suppose. But you'd better give your side of things. I warn you now, though. We have about forty-five minutes before we're due on a transport aircraft, so please be concise."

Rob told the man everything. The engine failure. The sight of a hostile gang approaching the disused airfield. His decision that Bunny's life was in danger.

The sergeant scribbled his notes.

"So, you landed, and then what?"

"Bunny had already been hit."

"Bunny?"

"I'm sorry, that's what everyone called Flight Lieutenant Pater-Smith."

The man rolled his eyes. "Fine. But he was alive?"

"Yes. I used our pistols to scare off the attackers."

The sergeant paused in his note-taking. He studied Rob. "So, you took them all on single-handedly, with a Browning nine millimetre. Did you kill anyone, sir?"

Rob shook his head. "No, no. I simply fired at their vehicles, one of which they abandoned. They fled in a lorry. I think to get reinforcements. I suspect they overestimated how much ammunition we had."

"I see, and you stole that abandoned vehicle?"

"I commandeered it on behalf of the government, to transport a critically wounded officer."

The sergeant blinked at him. "Well, I'll just put down you stole it, if that's okay with you, sir." He made his note. "And then what?"

"I drove to Ramadi to find a hospital."

The man screwed up his face. "That's two hundred miles."

"I had no choice, sergeant. That side of the country is virtually deserted."

"And Mr Pater-Smith died along the way?"

"I was directed to a cottage hospital in Ramadi. A kind doctor did what he could, but Bunny died on his table. After that, I called Bunny's batman, Asu, who drove out to pick us up."

"You called his batman, sir? Why didn't you call your unit commander?"

"It sounds silly, but I didn't know the telephone number, and the operator didn't speak good enough English to help me. But I found a number in Bunny's pockets, and it turned out to be for the Levies mess. They got a message to Asu. He's a resourceful chap and very loyal, so I think he took it upon himself simply to come and get us."

The sergeant completed his notes and scanned back through the three pages he'd written.

"The name of the doctor, sir?"

"Garsa, and his wife, Adorina. I'm afraid I don't know their family name."

He wrote a couple of further lines at the end of the statement. "I will have to check with them. They are the only ones who could corroborate any of this."

"Of course."

The sergeant looked at his watch. "And I have a flight to Cyprus, so they'd better have a telephone. I'm not staying in this godforsaken place to chase over to bloody Ramadi."

The man left the room.

Rob sank his head into his hands.

As soon as the sergeant spoke with Garsa, the story would fall apart. He would surely mention that Asu arrived with Rob and that Asu had been shot.

Everything would be thrown into doubt. And instead of telling the truth, Rob would be dragged into a court martial.

"Shit, shit, *shit*," he muttered to himself.

They'd launch a full investigation. His mess room would be searched.

He needed something better to explain Asu's presence in Trebil.

He should have told the truth: Bunny was on the make. He had no family, anyway; his reputation hardly mattered. And attention would turn to the murderous prince and his loyal thugs.

But somehow Rob had contrived to ensure he was the one sweating in a police interview room.

"*Fool.*"

Minutes went by.

He stood up and went to the door. Opening it, he tentatively looked around. In the next room, he saw Asu, also sitting by himself.

He quickly opened the door. "Asu," he whispered. "Does Garsa know to say you weren't there?"

Asu shook his head. "I could not speak with him, sir."

Footsteps approached; Rob darted back into the room.

The sergeant reappeared. "Thank you for your time, Mr May. We're searching for a way of contacting this doctor of yours, but I don't hold out much hope. We will, of course, have to pass this file to the Foreign Office. The diplomatic service must be informed. But we have what we need from you."

"I'm free to go?"

"Yes, sir."

"And Asu?"

The man nodded and produced a pen. "You will have to sign the statements first, sir."

Rob stared at the signature fields at the bottom of each sheet. They appeared innocuous enough, but the enormity of what he was about to do made his hand shake.

He signed his false statements.

T he squadron planning room was empty.
Every chart and list of procedures had been
stripped from the wall.

The last of many crates sat on the hardstanding outside, presumably waiting for the next visit from an RAF Transport command aircraft.

Clive Nuffield appeared, walking from the flight line, with the last of the five Venoms behind him.

"May! Is it true?"

Rob nodded.

"Christ, what bad luck. He wasn't everyone's cup of tea, but no one deserves that. Shot by a gang of thieves?"

He stopped in front of Rob and studied him.

"How are you? Fit to fly? You look awful, and you're going to need to change those coveralls before the boss sees you."

"I need to clear out my room. And Bunny's."

"Well. Chop-chop, then. Small personal bag only for the transit. Everything else in the last open crate. Listen, it's two and a bit hours to Cyprus. Can you manage it? We've lost two Venoms already, and without Bunny, we'll be leaving a third one here. The boss will kill me if I tell him we have to leave a bloody fourth!"

"I'll be fine. Is there a flight plan?"

"I was going to ask you to draw it up. Good exercise and all that. But under the circumstances, how about I lead the formation?"

Rob nodded and made his way to the door that led through the hangar.

A couple of mechanics were sweeping the large, empty floor. The last of the Royal Air Force in Iraq, with brooms in hand.

The British leaving the country they'd created.

He crossed the immaculate floor and stepped out into the sunshine, heading for the officers' mess.

When he got to his corridor, he found Asu with a box full of photographs and trophies, standing by his door.

"Come in," Rob said.

His bed was neatly made, and all clothes were ironed and on hangers or in drawers.

"I see Malkuno has been at work."

"Yes, sir," Asu replied. "But he is gone now, sir."

"Gone where?"

"There is a farm that will employ Assyrians, but it is many miles west of here. A bus left this morning."

"And the families?"

Asu shook his head. "They remain here, sir. A few of us are organising food for the children. But eventually, I will have to go, too, sir. To Ramadi to help my uncle."

"You will work in the hospital?"

"Yes, sir. I think I will change my name, too." He smiled. "Just in case."

Rob looked at his arm, which was back in a sling under his tunic. "How are you?"

"It's fine, sir. I tell people I fell."

Rob pulled a small holdall out of his wardrobe and placed it on the bed.

He retrieved the satchel from under the bed, and hoisted it, with some effort, onto the bed.

He undid the leather straps. He and Asu peered in at the pile of small gold bars.

Rob lifted one out. He'd never held a gold bar in his life.

There was a stamp on one side: *CREDIT SUISSE.*

There must have been at least thirty bars, maybe more. He had no idea how much gold was worth, but if the weight of the satchel was anything to go by, this was a small fortune.

"You must take the gold, Asu. I have no use for it."

"No, sir," Asu replied immediately.

"You must, Asu. To help your friends and family. To feed the children. Think what this gold could do for you."

Asu shook his head. "No, sir. There is nothing I can do with gold bars. I will be killed by the first man who hears of them. In your hands or an Iraqi's hands, sir, they are valuable. But not in the hands of an Assyrian."

Reluctantly Rob acknowledged this reality. He stuffed the valuable cargo at the bottom of his holdall.

Asu moved the box of Bunny's possessions to the bed. "I think this must go back to England, sir."

"What will I do with it?"

Rob examined the meagre possessions. On top was a photo frame on its front. He picked it up.

A black-and-white family photograph.

An officer and his wife, each holding a baby in flowing christening gowns.

A familiar but younger man with RAF wings.

He heard a noise and turned to see the door closing behind the departing Asu.

31

Rob could have taken the underground to Oval and walked, but it was a warm August day, and he needed the air.

The RAF Club was a stuffy, formal place to stay the night, and he regretted not splashing out for a hotel. He also wished he hadn't worn his uniform for this house visit. But it was too late to change that.

He crossed Green Park, heading for the river as Big Ben chimed out five o'clock.

His journey the previous day had taken him past Parliament and to Tower Bridge on the far side of the City. The buildings were blackened with decades of soot, and the national landmarks were in dire need of a scrub. But with the country limping from one economic crisis to another, he guessed no prime minister wanted to be accused of frivolous and unnecessary spending.

His business in the City followed a series of cautious phone calls, operating a long way from his area of expertise. But the transaction was uneventful, and Rob had a glimpse into another world, where deals for tens of thousands of pounds happened many times a day.

It was a pleasant evening. Families were in the parks, men and women fresh from a day's work, unwinding in the gentle English heat.

Eventually, he came to his chosen point to cross the river: Vauxhall Bridge.

Once over, he consulted his folded map.

He had resisted marking it. He was being overly cautious, but he didn't want questions from a fellow officer about why he was visiting a south London flat on a Friday evening.

He crossed under the railway line at Vauxhall, through dirty and smelly arches, feeling self-conscious in his day uniform. He was pleased to see a few other military men, scurrying home.

It didn't take him long to find Usborne Mews. It was considerably easier to navigate when walking at a few miles per hour rather than flying at four hundred knots.

The street was down on its luck; the once-grand Georgian townhouses had been converted into multiple small flats.

Rob stepped into the road as a woman pushed a pram past him, admonishing a small boy in school shorts.

He looked carefully, but it wasn't her.

Halfway down the street was an old front door with a modern set of bells, one for each flat.

Rob pressed 2A.

As he waited, he looked around to see a man in a flat cap and dark, baggy suit, leaning up against a bicycle, watching him from the road.

Rob tapped his feet and wondered how long he'd give it.

Noises came from within. Someone emerging down a flight of stairs.

The door opened.

It was her.

She wore a thin jersey and a black miniskirt.

Rob wasn't prepared for how young and attractive she would be.

"Mrs Pater-Smith?"

32

The flat was small, clean, and ordered. A living area ran into an open kitchen with a single bedroom off to the side. Enough space for one person to live comfortably.

But sitting cross-legged on the floor, with school books open, were two young teenage girls in blue gingham school dresses. Two straw boaters were hung neatly on the wall above them.

"Josephine and Helena," their mother said, introducing them.

The girls gave a bright hello to Rob and offered their hands. Immaculate manners.

"Hello. I'm Flying Officer Rob May. How do you do?"

He knew from the black-and-white photograph they must be twins, but they weren't identical. One was taller, with a freckled face; the other, darker-haired, with a pale complexion. He studied them for a second, looking for signs of his old flight commander.

"How do you do? Did you know our father?" the shorter girl asked.

"Josephine!" her mother admonished.

Rob looked up. She stood behind the girls and silently shook her head, leaving Rob unsure how to reply.

"I'll talk to your mother first if that's okay?"

The girls looked disappointed, but they picked up their school books and headed into the bedroom, closing the door behind them.

"I'm not sure what you're here to say," said Mrs Pater-Smith. "But I told the girls he died in a plane crash. It felt less awful than the truth."

"I understand."

"Tea, Mr May?"

"Yes, please, Mrs Pater-Smith. One sugar."

"Actually I use Dransfield now," she said as she walked up two steps to the small kitchen. "Have done for years. But you can call me Margery."

"Thank you, Margery. Please call me Rob."

The afternoon summer sun streamed through a bow window overlooking the street. Margery brought a tray into the living area, handing him a cup as she placed the tray on a small table in the centre of the room.

She gestured for Rob to sit in an armchair with his back to the window.

"Thank you," he said, placing his cap on the arm. "You didn't want the girls to keep their father's surname?"

Margery stirred a spoon of sugar into her tea. She looked so much younger than Bunny. No doubt life had aged him, but it was hard to imagine them together.

"It's complicated," she said after a pause. "So, is this unofficial business?"

"You received Bunny's possessions?" Rob asked. Then immediately followed up. "I'm sorry, did you call him Bunny?"

Margery laughed. "Everyone called him Bunny!"

Rob scanned the room for the photograph, but couldn't see it anywhere.

Margery leant back in her chair. "To be honest, I don't talk about him much. The girls don't remember him." She took a deep breath. "And I prefer not to be reminded."

Rob nodded and carefully put his tea down on the low table.

"I flew with Bunny. In Iraq. I was with him . . . at the end."

She didn't react at first. Then casually sipped her drink.

"They told me it was a gang of thieves."

Rob nodded. "It was."

"Hmm. I assumed he'd meet his end at the hands of a jealous husband," she said with an air of nonchalance. "Or jealous wife, for that matter."

Rob stared at her, just for a moment. A flash of conversation from Iraq came to mind. A gibe from a pilot about Bunny's predilections.

He shook his head. "Nothing like that. But I can't say he wasn't at least partially responsible for the situation in which he found himself. He made some bad choices."

"What does that mean?"

Rob had rehearsed this conversation in his mind. He'd assumed he would be nervous at causing more upset, but Margery seemed relaxed to the point of indifference.

"He wasn't exactly where he was supposed to be," Rob said, "and one thing led to another." He changed the subject. "It's funny. Bunny told me he wasn't married."

"'Funny'?" She tilted her head.

"I'm sorry, I didn't mean it like that . . ."

She smiled. "It's fine. It doesn't surprise me. We never

got divorced, because that would have involved him acknowledging us and actually having a conversation."

"When did you last speak to him?"

"November 1945."

Rob suppressed his shock. He guessed they were estranged, but she hadn't seen him since the war? *Twelve years.*

"The girls were seven months."

He thought about the photograph. It must have been around that time.

"I know it's none of my business . . " Rob began.

Margery puffed out her cheeks. "I don't mind telling you. But the girls don't know any of this." She got up and moved to a wireless that sat on an occasional table by the bedroom door. She turned a black dial, which made a satisfying click, and then waited for the set to warm up. Eventually some stringed classical music faded up.

She sat back down and drummed her fingers on the arm of her chair.

"We married in 1938. I was sixteen. We'd been going out since I was fourteen. He was a couple of years older than me. It doesn't sound a lot, but it was then. My parents hated the idea, of course. But he somehow won them over, as he won me over. It might be hard to believe, but he was enormous fun in those days."

Rob recalled Bunny's moments of eccentricity between the bouts of bullying and depression. The impromptu pre-dinner drinks.

"I can imagine it."

"Yes, well. I adored him. In the end, even my parents came to love him, despite their horror at the engagement. It was a happy time in my life. I thought I'd hit the jackpot. Had no idea that was the high point." She sipped her tea.

"Anyway, he was obsessed with aeroplanes. Which was fine. Fun, even. He used to drive me to Hounslow to watch them land."

"Sounds like my childhood." Rob smiled. He'd often begged his father to drive to Gatwick or London Airport.

"A month after we married, he walked to Uxbridge to join the RAF. It seems ridiculous to say, but I hardly saw him again."

"Really?"

She shook her head. "At first, I knew where he was, and he came home from time to time. But none of us was invited to his passing-out ceremony."

"What about his parents?"

"His mother died a couple of years before we met. He didn't tell me at the time, but I found out later she'd killed herself. That must have been hard for a sixteen-year-old."

Rob observed her. A hint of sympathy, maybe? Was there any affection left?

"Anyway, after Cranwell, he was all over the place, learning to fly. He came home at Christmas for two days. His mother left him some money, so he put a down payment on this flat. We moved in here. Or rather, I moved in."

"You didn't join him when he got his first posting?"

"I didn't even know where his posting was. I mean, he drove up sometimes. He mentioned Wittering once and Tangmere, but God knows where he slept at night. Or who he slept with."

"It must have been hectic training to be a pilot in '38 and '39," Rob said. "They knew war was coming."

"Maybe." She looked at the ceiling and clicked her tongue, apparently giving this idea some thought. "He loved the RAF then, but that changed. He changed."

"In what way?"

"Something happened to him. He went to France in early 1940. January, I think. Came home in the summer. That's when I noticed. He was here less than a month. Quiet. Barely out of bed some days. It wasn't completely out of character. He had his moods before the war, his dark side, his brother called it. But there were also fun times. War must have changed the balance. Once, when my parents came to visit, he sat in his pyjamas. It was excruciating for me. Then, one night in July, he left. I was out. Just came home to see his kit bag missing and the bed made."

Rob shook his head. "How awful for you."

Margery got up and headed into the kitchen. She returned with a packet of cigarettes and offered one to Rob.

"Thank you," he said, pulling a Rothmans from the blue-and-white paper case. She took an elaborate lighter in the shape of a bull from the table and lit it for him.

Margery slumped back into her seat. She kicked off her shoes and tucked her legs beneath her, then lit her cigarette, taking a long first drag.

"I don't mean to upset you, Margery."

"It's fine. It's been awhile since I've spoken to anyone about it. The girls don't know any of this. Anyway, it got worse and more complicated, if you can imagine. I bumped into a friend of ours in town, in August. He told me Bunny was at Duxford. I suppose he was fighting during the Battle of Britain time, although no one's ever told me. He came home again in November for a few days and then at Christmas. I tried to talk to him about his moods, but he didn't want to speak. He told me he had to go to Africa, and that was it for a long while. He dropped in less and less."

"What did you do? All by yourself?"

She fixed him with a stare. "I wasn't always by myself."

Rob tried not to change his expression. He'd been

brought up to believe marriage was sacrosanct, and yet who could blame a young wife effectively abandoned by her uncommunicative husband?

"Did you know Bunny was a twin?"

Rob raised both eyebrows. "He never mentioned it, but then I didn't know him very long."

"Boo," she said.

Rob couldn't help smiling. "Bunny and Boo."

She laughed as well. "Ridiculous, isn't it? An eccentric family. Childhood names that stuck with them for life."

"I don't know whether anyone at Habbaniya knew Bunny's real name," Rob said. "I didn't know it until I saw the paperwork that came with this address."

Margery laughed. "It is a ridiculous name, isn't it? I don't blame him for hanging onto Bunny. Boo's real name was far more prosaic, Roger. But it's what I called him—it felt more personal between us. And Roger Pater-Smith was a very different character. More strait-laced. Bunny was always a bit of a rogue. When I met them, they were inseparable. One of the hardest things for Bunny was that war took him away from Roger. It was harder for him than not seeing me. Roger was an apprentice in the city, but when war broke out, he joined the Royal Engineers. And it just so happened that whenever Bunny got leave, Roger was away and vice versa.

"He used to look in on me when Bunny was away. He'd bring me stuff when rations were low. He started staying longer. We started talking more. It wasn't deliberate . . ." She tailed off into a moment of thought.

"It wasn't deliberate," she repeated with more assertiveness. "But as Bunny drifted away, Roger drifted in. He was a friend just when I needed one."

Rob thought again about the black-and-white photograph. Now unsure whether that was Bunny or his brother. "It became something more than friends?"

She nodded, staring at the carpet, lost in a moment.

"As I say, none of this was planned. It just happened. It was the war, right? Everyone blames the war, I know, but hey ho, that's what it was. Christmas Day, 1943. God knows where Bunny was. My parents had moved out of London during the Blitz, and I didn't want to go to Bunny's father's house by myself. So I volunteered for work. I did a shift at the hospital in the morning. About three in the afternoon, Roger turned up. I was so surprised. And delighted. We had some tea, then some Christmas brandy. And he stayed the night."

The sun went behind a cloud and the room darkened. But Margery had a smile on her face. "It was rather wonderful. Strange, but wonderful. It was the middle of the war. You lived for the moment. Nothing felt like it had consequences. And every meeting with a man in uniform might be the last time you saw him alive. Roger was kind to me. Reliable, attentive. Everything Bunny had stopped being. We carried on seeing each other. He used his contacts to track Bunny's location. We knew he was coming back to England in May 1944, so the weekend before, Roger took me to Brighton. We walked hand in hand on the prom like we were married."

She took another deep breath.

"A few days later, Bunny came home. Worse than ever. Dark and angry. I came close to telling him about us, but Roger was against it. He was afraid Bunny would kill himself."

"Did you ever tell him?"

"Not outright. But I wonder whether he knew, anyway. He accused me of having affairs one night. But he was drunk. That's the only time he said something. But it was the day I'd made up some excuse and met Roger in the park. Whether I admitted it to myself at the time, it was a full-blown affair. I hated that. I begged Roger to come back with me to let him know. I wanted to be released from this awful marriage. But he stood firm. He said we should wait until the war's over. Then they both disappeared. The last day of May 1944."

"Just before D-Day?"

She nodded. "Yes. Obvious, I suppose, now. But it was a well-kept secret. Bunny left in the morning. I immediately telephoned Roger, but he had his own orders. I'm ashamed to say I dashed over there, anyway. I remember clearly, sitting on the train, smiling. For the first time I admitted something to myself. I was in love. Madly, deeply in love with Roger. My husband's brother, but it was like it was meant to be. That two people who perfectly fitted into each other's worlds had found each other. On the one hand it was a mess, but on the other, it was perfect. I felt so happy. We had the most amazing couple of hours together. He promised we would tell Bunny. I would ask for a divorce. He would support me." She looked up at the ceiling. Rob watched as she blinked back tears. "But of course, none of it happened."

Rob stayed silent, allowing her to deal with the moment. He didn't know the story, how could he? But he guessed what was coming.

Margery brushed a couple of tears from her skirt. "A week later, Bunny and Roger's father was on the doorstep when I returned from the shops. I saw him from a hundred yards and knew straightaway why he was here. I just kept saying to myself, 'Please let it be Bunny . . . please be Bunny.' How awful of me."

"It's understandable," Rob said.

She fished a tissue from a skirt pocket.

"Roger died on the beach. I can't remember any more. I can't remember a thing after that. I just sobbed. I can't imagine what he made of me. I suppose he just thought we were close in-laws."

"I'm so sorry."

She shook her head. "It was devastating for me. And to make it worse, I knew at some point, Bunny would come back. And there would be no Roger for me to run to. And then the cream on the cake. I found out I was pregnant."

"Roger's?"

She looked up and put the tissue away. "Of course. How could it have been Bunny's, if you know what I mean? He obviously knew that as well. He arrived back in July for a week. A dark, awful, week. Now it was my turn to be angry. I let him have it with both barrels. Told him how pathetic he'd been. But Bunny being Bunny, he simply went into himself. Arguing with him was impossible. I was so relieved when he disappeared again. I actually heard him on the phone begging for a posting to the Far East. Anything to get away from me, I suppose."

Rob looked around the flat again, searching for any sign that Bunny once lived there.

"There was a photograph? In Bunny's possessions? I assumed it was him with the babies?"

"It was. The twins were born in April 1945. I didn't know there would be two until a couple of days before. I was always told twins skipped a generation, but not in this case. Bunny was away, of course. His father knew nothing of what had been going on, and I certainly wasn't going to tell him. He was in a bad way when I called with the babies. Roger's death hit him hard, and he wasn't well. But his eyes lit up at the sight of the girls, and he insisted on organising a bloody family christening. I couldn't say no. So, in November, I took them on the train to Guildford. And Bunny was there. It was so awkward, but he put on this outer layer of frivolity for the day. Tried to make himself the centre of attention. A diversion, now that I look back. Anyway, he came home for . . ." She screwed up her face, trying to force the memory out. "For maybe a fortnight after that. The babies were demanding. Double trouble when it's twins. He was completely useless, and I was exhausted the whole time. When he left, I honestly felt relieved. That was May 8th, 1945."

Rob immediately recognised the date. "VE Day?"

"I think he went out to get drunk. I never saw him or heard from him again."

Rob shook his head. "What a thing to go through. You haven't remarried?"

"I can't, can I? I'm still technically married. Or I was until one of your colleagues came knocking last year."

Margery got up, cleared up the mugs, and headed into the kitchen. It was no more than a one-bedroom studio. He assumed she slept on the settee.

"If you don't mind me asking, I was wondering how you're coping now, all alone with the twins."

She turned and faced him from the kitchen. "It's hard. This place isn't big enough, and those two eat me out of house and home. My parents used to help, but Dad died and left little for Mum to live on. Bunny and Roger's father died about five years ago. I doubt there was much inheritance. But if there was, I'm assuming Bunny got it and spent it. So now it's just me and whatever social security money I can get. I own the flat now at least, but I can't get a mortgage on a bigger place. I don't earn enough. Most of the time we scrape by, but I still skip the odd meal to make sure they get what they need."

"Really?"

"If it means I can get the girls another school book. Why should they suffer because of him? The only thing I care about is that they get the best start in life I can provide them."

Rob drummed his fingers on the arm of the chair.

"I might be able to help."

Margery stopped clearing up and turned to face him, hands on hips. "You? Why?"

"I think your daughters have been cooped up long enough. Shall we go for a walk?"

33

The twins came out of the bedroom, claiming to have finished their homework. Margery quizzed them before allowing them to start dinner.

"We're going for a walk," she announced. The girls' heads swivelled and their eyes widened.

"Ooh, I see!" said the taller girl, who Rob thought was Helena.

Margery tutted and smiled. "Not like that," she said with some emphasis.

The girls looked at each other and giggled.

MARGERY LED Rob back towards the river, turning right, then left, and entering a small park.

"It's the nearest green bit," she said.

Rob turned to her. "If you could, would you move to the countryside with the girls?"

She shrugged. "It was impossible to do anything when Bunny was alive and refusing to answer letters. But now, I don't know. They seem settled at school."

"May I ask whether Bunny himself left you anything?"

"One hundred twelve pounds and a few pennies. A solicitor called a few months after he died. That was it. Don't get me wrong. It was extremely welcome. We bought a car, and the girls got new uniforms."

She stopped her amble and faced him. "So, Mr May. You've kept me in suspense long enough."

Rob, reached into his inside jacket pocket and pulled out an oblong piece of paper. He handed it to her and watched for a reaction.

Her mouth dropped open. She swallowed.

"This is from Bunny?"

"Yes. It's for you and the girls."

She stared at the money order without talking for ten seconds.

Slowly, she looked up.

"Nine thousand pounds! Did he steal this?"

Rob looked around them and then back at Margery. "I promise you, it was his money at the time he died, and for complex reasons I can't go into, I cannot do anything with it myself. I can't declare it, or hand it in to anyone without opening a very large can of worms. Believe me, I've been thinking about this for a very long time. There is no better place for it." He pointed at the order. "I'm sorry. I had it made out to Margery Pater-Smith. I hadn't realised you'd changed your name."

"That's not official," she said, still staring at the amount. "The bank account is still in my married name."

Rob smiled. "What will you do?"

Finally, Margery allowed herself a smile. "I don't know. I'm still getting over the shock! For one thing, we can eat meat more than twice a week."

Her face contorted and she burst into tears.

Rob whipped out a handkerchief.

"I'm sorry," she said sobbing. "It's been so hard."

"Of course. You're in shock."

"I've been stuck in no man's land. I couldn't move on. But this . . . It changes everything."

"I'm glad. Now, fold it up so you don't lose it. I think you'll want to visit the bank first thing tomorrow. If they ask, and they probably will, you simply tell them it's an inheritance from your late husband."

She looked down at the paper again, then back up at Rob, gathering herself. "Would you at least stay for dinner?"

"Thank you, but no. I'm back to my squadron tomorrow, and I have one more appointment today."

She looked at him. "None of this feels real."

"Believe me, nothing about my time with your husband felt real to me."

34

Lambeth Palace was hard to get into.

What looked like the main entrance—an ornate wooden door—was sealed shut. There was no bell to ring, and his fist made only a feeble sound when he tried to knock.

"Flying Officer May?" a voice called from behind him.

He turned to see a clergyman in round NHS glasses, carrying a wad of paper. He held out a hand.

"Hello, I'm Michael Litherland. My assistant told me you'd be calling. I'm sorry, but I have only a couple of minutes."

"That's quite all right. Thank you for seeing me. I believe you are coordinating help for former members of the Assyrian Levies. Your name appears on the charity register as the chairman."

"Indeed. As you probably know, it's a favoured cause of the archbishop. We have a small team, doing what we can."

"This may sound like a silly question, but would money help you?"

Michael Litherland burst out laughing. "We get nothing but the occasional encouraging word from the Foreign Office. We rely entirely on donations. So, yes. You could say money helps."

"Good. I'd like to donate."

The vicar looked surprised. "I see. On behalf of yourself?"

"Actually, it's in the name of a former colleague. He lost his life in Iraq a year ago."

"I'm sorry to hear that."

"Thank you. But he was close to his batman. An Assyrian man called Asu. I was rather hoping you might find him."

The vicar looked bemused. "Do you have any other names for Asu?"

"Everything I know is on the piece of paper with the money order. I had it made out to the name of the charity. Will that be okay? I can get it redone, but there might be a delay."

"That will be fine, thank you."

Rob delved back into his inside jacket pocket and pulled out a white envelope.

"It's rather a lot."

Litherland raised an eyebrow. "How much?"

"Nine thousand, two hundred and seventy one pounds."

Litherland took a sharp breath and nodded. "Well. In that case, I know the archbishop will want to thank you personally—"

"That won't be necessary. The only thing he must know, is the money came from an Royal Air Force pilot with a distinguished service record and someone who wanted to give something back to the men who so loyally served him."

"I see. And this gentleman's name?"
"Flight Lieutenant Augustus Pater-Smith."

THE END

ALSO BY JAMES BLATCH

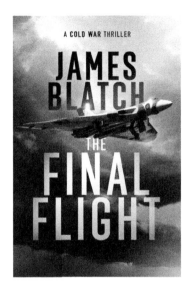

The Final Flight

A deadly crash, a government conspiracy, a lone pilot with one chance to uncover the truth.

Turn the page for a taste of The Final Flight.

THE FINAL FLIGHT
FRIDAY 10TH JUNE, 1966

Susie Attenborough sat naked in a tent. Legs crossed, in her unzipped sleeping bag.

She stretched before fumbling through a pile of clothes to find her wristwatch.

5.45AM.

The sun had been up for forty minutes; the thin canvas did little to keep the light out.

She wound the watch for a new day. Outside in the nearby hedgerow and copse, the dawn chorus was underway. She savoured the gentle birdsong, knowing it would soon be replaced by howling jet engines.

Susie yawned, climbed over the detritus of her clothes out into the daylight.

Her bare feet felt cold on the dewy grass. Rabbits hopped around the taxiway on the other side of the high security fence, their lower portions disappearing into a sliver of mist.

The peace camp was still. Her eyes swept over the other tents, scattered around the central wigwam. Silently she counted them, checking for new arrivals, until she caught sight of a man: tall with a beard, bare chested in cut-off shorts. He smiled back at her.

Susie recognised him from an introduction when she'd first arrived. David?

As it wasn't normal behaviour to stand around stark naked in the UK countryside, even at a peace commune, she put one arm over her breasts and the other between her legs and awkwardly backed into the tent.

She took her time in pulling on her clothes: a short skirt and a white blouse.

When she re-emerged, David was gone, but a few more campaigners had emerged from their burrows. She exchanged smiles before heads turned at the sound of a deep rumble reverberating from the airfield.

She checked her watch; barely 6AM.

She wandered over to the fence and looked toward the three large green hangars at the other end of the runway. A few aircraft were out already and one, with propellers turning, was the source of the noise.

A movement caught her eye: a Land Rover with a canvas hood over its back, speeding around the peritrack, heading their way. She stood her ground as the vehicle passed her, just a few feet the other side of the wire.

The driver and passenger glanced in her direction. She noted the green lining on their caps but couldn't place the uniform.

Since her arrival, all the talk had been about when they would come for them, armed with an eviction notice.

So far they'd been left alone.

She knew that would change once the direct action began.

———

Millie arrived at TFU with a plan. A vague, not-thought-through plan. But at least it was a plan.

The map tables were empty as the pilots and some navs were at the morning weather brief.

He walked over to the admin office and ensured the Vulcan they were allocated was not needed too soon after they were due to return.

Rob appeared along with other aircrew as the met brief broke up.

Millie fixed an amiable look on his face. Rob looked nervous, but he greeted him loudly and asked if he wanted a tea.

He accepted the offer and his face brightened. They moved to the tea bar together and Millie kept up the conviviality, chatting about the cricket.

"Sobers was magnificent at Lord's apparently. One hundred and sixty-three not out."

Rob looked a little uncertain, as if he wasn't sure what was going on. But he joined in.

"It'll be hard for us to win the match from here."

"Indeed," said Millie. He paused and put a hand on Rob's back. "It's better to be on good terms, isn't it?"

"It is."

Speedy Johnson announced himself in the room and Millie took them over to a planning table. He spread out a chart that covered most of Northern England with the dramatic brown relief of the Lake District prominent in the top-left corner.

He pointed at the middle of the hills. "The Lakes. We need some big dips below us."

Speedy peered at where Millie's finger had landed.

"Wales has dips, famous for it. And it's a lot closer."

Millie nodded. "It does, but we need to cover as much

different terrain as possible. We've done Wales a lot recently. Time for a change of scenery."

Speedy shrugged. "All good with me. It'll give Brighty something new to plan."

Rob kept quiet.

The group broke up and Millie found Steve Bright to brief him before moving to the admin office. While the flight lieutenant stood over him, he withdrew eight blank tapes from the secure cabinet, placing the cardboard sleeves into his flight case.

———

An hour later, Millie stood on the edge of the TFU apron in his flying coveralls, helmet on, his oxygen mask hanging loosely by his chin.

He realised he was pacing and made an effort to keep his feet planted, concentrating on the ballet of manoeuvring aircraft in front of him.

A roar caught his attention and he watched an English Electric Lightning thunder along the runway. Its silver wings glinted in the sunshine as the pilot pulled it into a vertical climb and rolled around three hundred and sixty degrees. He smiled as the aircraft became a small silver dart and disappeared into a layer of cloud.

A moment later, Steve, Speedy and Rob appeared by his side and they walked toward the white, delta-winged Vulcan. Speedy climbed in while Rob set off around the aircraft, peering into the undercarriage recesses and checking various nooks and crannies.

Millie followed Steve Bright into the rear bay and settled in.

After agreeing that Bright would carry out the post

hatch checks, he strapped himself in and set about organising the tapes.

He removed one from its sleeve and pre-loaded it, glancing across at the navigator as he did so. It wasn't so unusual, but ordinarily he loaded the reels only when needed during the flight.

Steve Bright was busy with his own preparation; a longer trip to a less visited part of the country for the young navigator.

Rob's head appeared in the hatchway.

"Ready to go?"

"Yep!" the navigator replied.

Rob climbed the next few steps into the cockpit and Bright checked the hatch was closed and latched.

They brought the Vulcan to life. The pilots weren't on the intercom yet, but he could hear them proceeding through the various checklists.

Ticking sounds and various mechanical whirrings preceded the familiar spooling up of the engines.

A few minutes later, they bounced along the runway before the aircraft pitched up and Millie and Bright were pressed forward against their straps.

Millie moved a hand forward and flipped the master switch on the Guiding Light panel.

It was unusual to power the system up so early. He knew the smaller repeater panels in the cockpit would also come to life; he could only hope neither Speedy or Rob would pay any attention to them at this stage in the flight.

He started the tape running.

After twenty minutes, an orange indicator blinked out and it was time to switch to a fresh tape.

Millie opened the metal flap over the reels; his hand was trembling.

He removed the full take-up reel, then switched the empty reel onto the take-up spindle. He reached down and retrieved a new blank reel from his flight bag.

In his peripheral vision, it seemed like Steve Bright was looking at him.

He glanced across, but in fact Bright was staring at his chart with his finger poised on the next waypoint.

Millie quickly dropped the new tape onto the spindle, closed the flap and restarted the data recorder.

He sat back, relieved.

The change took ten seconds; it had felt like ten minutes.

He put a white sticky label on the reel and marked it, simply *BLANK 'A'*.

A nonsense label that meant something only to him.

He retrieved a brand new pocket-sized notepad and opened it, noting down the date, time and location for the recording. He paused for a moment; even this note could be used against him at some point. After hesitating, he completed the entry anyway. There was no way around it.

He looked at his watch and checked the navigation plan. He had time for two reels more before they reached the entry gate.

Sitting back, he let the static whine from the intercom wash over him. It was warm inside from the time the aircraft had sat on the ground. He closed his eyes.

"You still with us, Millie?" called Steve Bright.

Millie woke.

"Falling asleep in a nuclear bomber? And we're only going to Keswick, chap. Not Vladivostok."

Millie looked at his stopwatch. Eighteen and a half minutes gone. Time to change reels again.

As he removed the second tape, Steve Bright turned to him again.

"We're not there yet, Millie."

He felt a spike of adrenaline in his stomach.

He looked up and smiled. "I know, just making sure we're ready."

Bright gave him a thumbs up.

Had Rob heard the exchange on the intercom?

Fourteen minutes later, they began their descent, and Millie swapped out the second reel, taking advantage as Steve Bright's attention switched to the nav-radar.

He quickly marked up his second tape and loaded the first of the official reels for today's run.

The Vulcan settled at one thousand feet straight and level. Millie glanced at his copy of the route. They should be about twenty miles north of Bassenthwaite Lake. He felt a jolt as Guiding Light engaged. The ride became bumpy as the computer, with none of the finesse of a human, mirrored the contours of the ground beneath them.

"Tape running, Millie?" Rob called over the intercom.

"Roger," Millie confirmed.

The ride became more undulating as they continued deeper into the valleys and hills of the Lake District. In the dark confines of the rear crew area, Millie started to feel nauseous.

After nineteen minutes of being heaved around, he was able to occupy himself briefly, changing another reel. As they passed the thirty-minute mark and began to climb out, he changed once more.

He had two official tapes to enter into the system, and he was onto his third unofficial tape.

On the transit home, he recorded one more reel, labelling the four sleeves *BLANK 'A', 'B', 'C' and 'D'.*

Ten minutes out, as they descended into the West Porton circuit, he powered down the Guiding Light panel, loosened his straps and tried to stretch in the limited space.

————

Susie watched the white jet sweep directly overhead, her eyes following its wide arc around the airfield. The plane's landing gear unfolded as it travelled south before banking again, lining up to land.

It arrived over the fence and she watched it descend toward the runway, where it seemed to loiter in the air for a while before finally settling on its wheels with a screech and a puff of smoke.

David and his bushy beard appeared next to her.

"They take off heading that way and land coming back," he said.

"Wind. It must have changed during the day."

"Ah, I see. And that's a Victor, I think."

"Avro Vulcan," she corrected him.

He raised his eyebrows. "No, I think the Vulcan looks different, has a high tail at the back."

"The Victor is the one with the high tail, David. The white aircraft that's just landed is an Avro Vulcan. It's distinguished by its delta-shaped wing. Unique in bombers, I believe."

"Are you sure?"

"Yes, I'm sure, David. It's a bloody Vulcan." She smiled at him.

"Hmm."

She laughed. "Sorry. Don't mean to sound bossy. I grew up with three brothers and a father in the Navy. I can identify most cars, ships and planes. I could probably name you the England team for the World Cup as well."

"A tomboy? Fair enough."

They headed back toward the tents.

"So, David, what are we doing here? I mean, I know we're a protest camp, but what are we actually going to do?"

He reached into the back pocket of his shorts, produced a small packet of tobacco and began rolling a cigarette.

"Keen, aren't you?"

"Just don't want to waste my time."

He studied her. "Well, we're alerting the world to a new technology that's doing god knows what with aircraft capable of dropping nuclear bombs."

"OK, but that sounds rather... passive."

He smiled at her.

"Maybe, but it's important. We're also disrupting the military as they prepare for an unthinkable and unwinnable war."

"How?"

"What do you mean, 'how'?"

"How are we disrupting the military? I mean, we haven't exactly shut down anything or stopped anything happening, as far as I can see."

The smell of burning paraffin drifted over, and a noise rose from their left. They looked to see a dark grey Canberra taxiing. Inside the cockpit, the pilot looked directly at them, and Susie could have sworn he was laughing under his mask. She waited for the noise to dissipate, but as the aircraft turned onto the runway, the engines wound up into a scream. The Canberra rolled forward, disappearing behind trees.

Susie shrugged. "As I say, we don't appear to be disrupting very much."

He lit his cigarette.

"Well, we don't know that for sure. For a start, our very presence here is bringing attention—"

"We've got to do more than that, surely?"

"Let me finish. We're bringing attention to an installation the government seems desperate to keep out of the public's eye. Plus, they may have modified their behaviour. Do you think they would parade anything secret in front of us? We have no idea how much activity they have curtailed because we're here." He sucked on his cigarette. "You seem impatient, I hope you're not thinking of leaving us?"

She shook her head. "No. Well, I can't stay forever. It's just that if there's something going on that needs to be stopped, I think we should stop it. I didn't come here to watch planes."

He smiled at her before looking around.

"Not everything worthwhile involves a set of bolt croppers, Susie. Some things require a little more subtlety." He moved off toward the wigwam. "Patience is a virtue."

————

Back in the planning room, Millie sat at his desk, flight case by his feet.

He had already logged the two official reels into the project cabinet, leaving six in his bag, each filled with height readings from Guiding Light.

He tried to concentrate on some paperwork, but he found it hard. His eyes kept drifting down to the case containing the illicit reels.

He wanted to go to the loo, but was reluctant to leave it unattended.

"This is silly," he muttered to himself.

Kilton emerged from his office, in blue coveralls and

orange Mae West life jacket, holding his gloves and flying helmet.

"Ready?" he called over to a group of pilots at the tea bar. Rob left the group, also dressed to fly. The pair of them disappeared through the airfield door.

"Appraisal trip with the boss, apparently."

Millie looked up to find Jock MacLeish standing over him.

"Oh. Unusual, isn't it? For Kilton to take a junior pilot."

"Yes. But then Mark Kilton works in mysterious ways, Millie."

He helped MacLeish with his own project paperwork, instructing him on what could safely remain in his locker or case and what had to be placed in the secure cabinets.

"What would we do without you, Millie?" MacLeish said, and headed off to deposit his trial reports.

After lunch, Millie spent the afternoon on more admin, tea drinking and wondering how the hell he was going to smuggle Top Secret tapes out of the country's most secure Royal Air Force station.

———

Rob and Kilton arrived back at 2.30PM, a long time after they left for a simple check of a pilot's flying proficiency.

Rob was all smiles on his return; clearly it had gone well.

Millie kept an eye on the clock, trying to judge the best time to leave and avoid a random search.

Best when it's busy? Quiet? He couldn't recall many car searches after leaving the mess in the evening. They were generally carried out during the morning and evening rushes.

Jock MacLeish worked at a desk nearby.

"Hey, Jock. Are you heading to the mess tonight?"

"It's Friday, Millie. Need you ask?"

"Ah, of course. Happy Hour."

As soon after 4PM as they could get away with, a group left TFU heading to the mess.

Millie stood up, lifted his case, and walked to the door. The case suddenly felt heavy in his hand and he was conscious of every step he took.

He left the planning room and walked the few yards toward the door that opened out into the car park. As he got closer, it swung open and the commanding officer of the RAF West Porton security police walked in.

The man, in smart light blue uniform with green stripes on his sleeves and cap, walked directly toward him.

Millie held his breath, but the officer brushed past him without making eye contact.

He exhaled and headed to his car, placing his flight bag in the passenger footwell.

At the mess, he carefully locked every door before heading inside to the bar.

He spotted MacLeish sitting with the old men of the Maintenance Unit. The Scot waved and held up a pint for him.

Millie took his seat and clinked glasses.

JR, one of the MU pilots, looked as old as the aircraft they flew. His dark, sunken eyes seemed to swallow light. But there was a twinkle in his eye and Millie always enjoyed the old boys' company.

The beer tasted good.

The room filled with smoke and chatter. Millie spied Rob at the bar, surrounded by the senior test pilots.

Jock informed him that Rob and the boss had landed

away at Daedalus, a Navy base near Portsmouth. Had lunch together in the mess, apparently.

Around 8PM, several hours after he'd started drinking, Millie said his goodbyes and headed toward his car. He was a bit wobbly and realised he was not in the best state to cope with his first attempt to smuggle out a tape. Maybe the alcohol would provide Dutch courage.

After two attempts, he persuaded the Rover's engine to start. He steered through the full car park, peering across the playing-field toward the lights of the main gate.

There was one man on the barrier, maybe a corporal. In the hut next to him, a sergeant with a clipboard.

He got to the main road that ran through the middle of the domestic side of the station and turned left.

Slowing down, he willed the barrier to rise.

Nothing.

The sergeant, complete with clipboard, appeared by the side of his car.

Millie wound down the window.

The sergeant leant down to bring his head level.

"Good evening."

"Hello," Millie managed.

"Just a word of caution, sir. We've spotted protestors out and about tonight. Best not to stop on the way home."

"I wasn't planning to, Sergeant, but thank you for the tip."

The sergeant nodded, then appeared to scrutinise Millie, before he glanced at his car.

"You haven't had too much to drink, have you, sir?"

"Certainly not. Just one or two, Sergeant."

The man nodded again, but didn't change his expression. He raised himself back up and moved to the front of the hut.

After an age, the barrier slowly lifted.

Millie put the car into first gear, pushed the accelerator with his foot, released the clutch. The car lurched forward and stalled.

His heart pounded.

He waited for the sergeant to reappear, probably convinced that he was drunk.

Before he tried to restart the engine, he forced himself to pause. He put the car in neutral, left his foot on the clutch and turned the key.

It started.

This time, Millie made sure he pulled away with no further issues. He glanced into his wing mirror to see the sergeant staring, his image growing smaller.

ALSO BY JAMES BLATCH

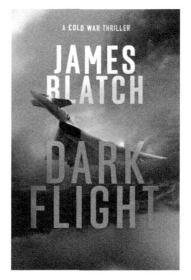

Dark Flight

In the dark recesses of a hangar, hidden deep in the Mojave desert, an experimental hypersonic aircraft waits for a secret, dangerous and highly illegal mission.

Sign up for news of future James Blatch novels:

jamesblatch.com

HISTORICAL NOTE ABOUT DESERT VENOM

Desert Venom came about after a research visit to the National Records Office at Kew in London. Of the dozen files I ordered, one stood out. In bright red and marked TOP SECRET, it contained an assessment of the deteriorating security situation at the Habbaniya Cantonment. This area was the home of members of the British Levies and their families.

The British Levies was established during the First World War and by the 1950s they had a specialist role serving the Royal Air Force at its two stations in Iraq; Habbaniya and Shaibah. Made up mainly by Assyrians (traditionally Christian) and some other minorities in Iraq including Kurds.

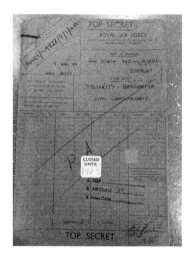

The file details hostility from both sides. Attacks on Assyrians from locals and an episode in which 'Moslem children' (sic) were excluded from the Habbaniya station primary school.

Against this deteriorating background, the UK Government was keen to renew the Anglo-Iraqi treaty which allowed them use of the bases. They also drew up secret plans to leave in a timely fashion.

As second file contained a fascinating set of correspondence between the Archbishop of Canterbury (Geoffrey Fisher) and the Prime Minister (Winston Churchill). The archbishop made the case for the resettlement of members of the Levies in the event that the treaty was not renewed. The letters were dated 1952 and 1953.

In the event, the treaty expired without renewal in October 1957. The British abandoned Habbaniya as well as thousands of their loyal Assyrian servants.

217 (Fighter) Squadron is fictitious but loosely based on 6 Squadron, which operated Venom's at Habbaniya until June 1956, when it relocated to Nicosia in Cyprus.

The haste in which the British left Habbaniya is exaggerated in this story. In reality, it was a swift operation, but not quite 'by the end of tomorrow' swift.

'Prince Nuri' is the fictitious brother of the real King Faisal II. In reality Faisal was a little young to have a younger brother of Nuri's stature. In fact Faisal came to the throne at the age of three and was just 22 in 1957.

The nearest real version of a Prince Nuri was Faisal's uncle, Abd al-Ilah, who acted as regent on his behalf and remained his close advisor once he came of age.

I portrayed Nuri as impetuous and ready for the fight in the face of an increasingly hostile military and political class in Iraq. In reality, Faisal and Abd al-Ilah had no fight in them. When the inevitable military coup took place on 14th July 1958, Faisal stood down his guard, allowing the army into the palace unopposed. Within minutes, Faisal, Abd al-Ilah, his wife, as well as several members of extended royal family were shot dead in the courtyard.

In a macabre final act, Faisal and his uncle's bodies were drawn naked through the streets of Bagdhad.

The country fell under a different sort of dictatorship which led, within a decade to the Ba'athists and the long and bloody reign of Saddam Hussein.

ACKNOWLEDGMENTS

As with my first novel, The Final Flight, my primary source for inspiration and authenticity was my father.

Flying Officer John Blatch was posted to RAF Habbaniya in 1954. He flew Venom FB.4s with 6 Squadron until an onward posting to Fighter Weapons School to become a Pilot Attack Instructor (Top Gun, thirty years before Maverick).

My father beside his Vampire at RAF Deversoir, Egypt in 1953

I have Dad to thank for numerous small details, such as the fuel regulator that was prone to fail on the Venom, the layout of the Habbaniya mess, the road 'Cheapside' that contained the tailors for RAF uniform through to his fond recollections of his Assyrian batman.

The month of this book's publication will see his 92nd birthday. He remains sharp minded and able bodied.

Dr Stuart Thorne helped me with the injuries in the story. I began by telling him Bunny needed to be shot then driven in the back of a Land Rover for 2.5 hours before saying a final few words and expiring. He devised a credible medical scenario for me.

I have a small but close group of writing friends. We call ourselves the Tiki Bar Pals after the bar where we first met. They are the best sounding board a writer could want and the best friends anyone could have. The character of Bunny became rounded and complex thanks to a discussion during a long drive from Tampa to Atlanta to escape Hurricane Ian in 2021. Lucy and Cecelia write romance, Nathan writes time travel noir (a genre I think he invented) and Boo writes powerful literary fiction. The common link is an empathy for their fellow man, particularly those who walk among us carrying invisible wounds. Bunny was not a bad person. He was a person with crippling depression in an age and position where acknowledgement of such would end his career; the only thing he truly loved.

Thank you to my erstwhile editors, Andrew Lowe and Leighton Wingate. My personal crack squadron of elite pilots.

Finally, this book is dedicated to my brother David. He died from an illness at the age of fourteen, I was twelve at the time. It was the darkest day of my life, but as the years go by the light David shone in our family has penetrated that traumatic shadow. David was funny, clever, talented and courageous in the face of health issues. He was a better person than me in every sense.